This story is a work of fiction. All names, characters, organisations, places, events and incidents are products of the author's imagination or are used fictitiously. Any resemblance to any persons, alive or dead, events or locals is entirely coincidental.

Text copyright © 2021 Ella Stone

Second edition published 2024

Paper Cat Publishing

ISBN: 979-8486044847

Edited by Carol Worwood

All rights reserved.

No part of this book should be reproduced in any way without the express permission of the author.

1

Narissa

I'd just like to point out that this is the first time I've ever woken up naked in the back of a jeep driven by a vampire who has just rescued me from certain execution. Suffice it to say, I don't always make the best life choices. This is not going to be your average road trip.

Clicking out the cricks in my neck, I try to figure out where we are. Outside, the sky is tinged tangerine, and the sun is well past its zenith. Barren hills with sheer, grey rock faces and sparse, brittle grass roll out as far as I can see. There's no wildlife on display. No deer or rabbits or even people walking their dogs. We're not in London anymore. That much is obvious.

"Everything all right?" Calin doesn't bother turning his gaze from the road as he speaks. I say "road". At one time, it must have been tarmacked. Now it's ninety percent potholes. Drawing my eyes away from the scenery, I turn my attention back to him to answer his question.

"Some clothes would be nice," I say.

"Of course," he replies, throwing me the quickest of glances in the rear-view mirror. "I picked up some things. They're in the plastic bag on the floor. I'm afraid the choice was somewhat limited."

I've never been bothered about clothes. Jeans and a vest top suit me fine. My change from summer to winter wardrobe generally consists of adding a hoodie on top of whatever I normally wear and occasionally putting on boots rather than trainers. However, there are jeans and there are jeans, and I know from first glance that whatever is in the bag is not going to be great. They are a swampy green with deliberately frayed hems, rhinestones on the pockets and at least two sizes too big. The T-shirt is a man's large size, though oddly baby pink in colour. On the plus side, the oversized clothes make it easier to manoeuvre myself into them under the blanket without completely exposing myself to Calin. Then again, given that he's seen me change back from a werewolf and obviously just carried me naked to the car, that ship has already sailed.

When I'm dressed, I squeeze myself through the gap between the two front seats and strap myself in. A hundred questions had been whirring around my head, but now I'm sitting here, there's not a single thing I can think of to say. Silence blooms between us. He got me out of there. He rescued me. And he had to kill his own kind to do it—vampires who knew him, worked with him. He murdered them to make sure I would be safe.

"We're in the Scottish Highlands, near Inverness," he says, finally. "It's still a way to go, I'm afraid."

"To the werewolf pack?"

"To the werewolf pack."

This is ridiculous. Completely crazy.

I, Narissa Knight, am a werewolf.

Shit. Nothing about this is okay. As I start to recall what happened before I was knocked unconscious, another thought strikes.

"Oliver?" I gasp, suddenly remembering my life wasn't the only one on the line last night. Oliver, my former best friend and member of Blackwatch, tried to rescue me. He came to Calin's flat, where Styx had laid a trap for me. Even after all the lies I'd told him and after everything with Rey, Oliver still came for me and tried to save me. "Is he … is he …" I can't bring myself to say the words. I'm already responsible for losing one of my best friends. If it's happened again …

"He's okay," Calin says, reading the worry in my voice. "Well, okay may be a slight exaggeration, but he'll survive. Grey going up against Styx says something. I have to admit, I admire him."

Styx: the vampire who murdered my father. The vampire I'd spent the last decade hunting. It's fair to say I was a little under-prepared when our paths finally crossed. If my animal instinct hadn't kicked in … I shudder at the thought, and the chill lingers.

I've got so much to process right now——I'm a werewolf. I want to file this inconvenient fact right at the back of my mind, along with a dozen other things I don't want to confront. But it's proving difficult. Ever since I came to, I've been able to feel the wolf, there beneath my skin. It's accompanied by a constant gnawing sensation, as if something is lurking in the back of my mind, waiting to be unleashed.

"How did it happen?" I ask, pulling the blanket over from the back seat. It's not cold. I just need the comfort right now. "How did I become ... that?"

The four-by-four groans into a lower gear as Calin takes a turn onto a muddy track. He's got no map or GPS, but he seems pretty confident in where he's going. Judging by the last time we saw a building or a service station, I'd say it's safe to assume these werewolves are big on privacy. Once again, Calin's eyes stay on the road as he speaks.

"I'm not an expert, but I know that vampire venom is what activates the werewolf gene and triggers the transformation," he says. "It can't happen without it. But the gene must have always been in you. I believe it comes from the mother's side."

"From my mother's side? So that means she was one, too?"

He shrugs. "I don't know. Not necessarily. She could have been like you but never had the gene activated."

"Wow."

More information to digest. Unfortunately, there's no chance of asking her. She died when I was three. I hope for her sake she never had to go through the pain of what just happened to me—bones breaking and muscles tearing apart before reforming into something new. Every single cell metamorphosing. Just thinking about it causes my skin to crawl. I clench my fists, trying to fight the clawing sensation that ripples through me once again. There's a growling inside my head, too. Crap. Crap. This is not normal. There is no way this is normal.

Forcing it all back down, I turn to Calin and ask one of the questions that I just can't switch off.

"How did I not know werewolves existed? My dad—and Oliver—never said a thing about them. Nothing whatsoever."

"Did they not?"

"No."

Not that my dad had been a massive talker. Notebooks were his thing. He had hundreds of them, little leather-covered journals he scribbled in religiously during the time he was employed at Blackwatch. By the time he was murdered, everything had gone digital, but he still wrote in his notebooks every night when he got home from work. It was a habit he just couldn't kick. Sometimes, I would peer over his shoulder while he drew sketches. Sometimes, when I was in my early teens, I would flick through them while I waited for him to get home from a late shift, although I was mostly interested in the pictures. He loved drawing. He could barely go two pages without adding some sort of illustration.

God, I wish he was still here. I don't even have the books to remember him by. When he was murdered,

Blackwatch swept in and cleared the place out before I'd had a chance to blink. I hated them for that. I hate them for a lot of reasons, actually, like refusing to believe me when I told them it was a vampire that had killed him. For refusing to help me find the monster and bring him to justice. It's strange, though. I know I didn't read everything he wrote, but he often used to talk to me about his job, and he never mentioned anything about werewolves. Not once.

"Our relationship with werewolves has always been difficult, complicated," Calin says. "Our joint history is, well, muddy at best and according to folklore goes back to when they were first created. And while we were hunting them down, to protect ourselves, humans were using them to hunt us. But their rapport with ordinary people was never good.

"Then came the Blood Pact and we finally made our peace with werewolves. It was agreed that we would supply them with the venom they need to activate their hidden gene—in extremely limited quantities—in return for which, they would not venture out of their territories. This suited them. They are an elusive bunch and have always sought anonymity. They were more than happy to be left alone. I suppose it's possible that, over time, humans just forgot about their existence. Either that, or Blackwatch simply didn't see them as a big-enough threat to monitor."

"Somehow, I think I might have changed that a little."

CHAPTER 1

I take his silence as agreement, although I don't dwell on the matter. Another thought has distracted me instead.

"If relationships between vampires and werewolves were strained, are you going to be safe?"

I may have only known him for a few weeks, but I really don't think I can be responsible for another friend getting hurt, or worse. Images of Rey and her final moments will haunt me for the rest of my life. It was my fault my best friend died. She sacrificed herself, outing herself as a witch to a room full of vampires so that I could escape them. Her hand, reaching out to me as they swarmed around her after she'd revealed her powers, her final cries, will never fade from my memory. Just as the sound of Oliver's bones crunching, as Styx threw him against the wall of Calin's flat never will, or my dad's neck snapping in his hands. They will be with me forever.

"It'll be fine," Calin says, bringing me round from the waking nightmare that plays on a loop. "I've never been to the camp, but I recently made the acquaintance of a member of the pack, in a nearby town."

I'm fairly sure that the word *nearby* is subjective in this context. There can't be a decent-sized town for at least fifty miles. Still, I ignore that for now.

"Made the acquaintance? What does that mean?"

"It's not a very interesting story. I bumped into one of them, that's all. Just after your first visit to me. I was here dealing with a rogue vampire problem."

Rogues. I remember them being the bane of Dad's life. One vampire, refusing to adhere to the Blood Pact could cause him weeks of paperwork. I'd never really considered the possibility that other vampires would go out to hunt them, though.

"So, what do you know about them? The pack?" I ask, trying not to let the last word stick in my throat.

"Very little. Our meeting was quite brief. I've contacted them again and explained the situation, and they're willing to take you in."

Willing to take me in. Wow, that sounds great, doesn't it? Really friendly and warm. But then, what other options do I have right now?

My next question comes out as a whisper.

"The vampires want me dead, don't they?"

"At the moment. But I'm going to talk to Polidori. Don't worry. We'll clear your name once they know what Styx did."

He glances my way, then reaches out and takes my hand. I clearly don't look convinced.

"Styx murdered your father. He lured you into a trap. He tried to kill you and Grey, too. All of that goes against the Blood Pact. He would have had to pay for his crimes."

"And what about the vampires guarding my cell and the rest of the Council building? They didn't have crimes to pay for."

"Maybe not but let me worry about that. Your job is to stay here and keep out of sight. And learn to be a wolf, I guess."

This last comment plunges us into another silence. Learn to be a wolf? What is that supposed to mean? Learn to howl at the moon? To chase rabbits? Do werewolves do that? And what about being part of a pack? The last thing I need is some burly alpha barking orders at me. Is that how it's going to be? Right now, I wouldn't count anything out.

The road has become stony and potholed and we lurch along. After a minute of fiddling with the radio, trying to get reception, I give up. Silence will have to do.

For over forty minutes, we stay that way, both of us alone with our thoughts. Mine flicker around the same topics. My mother, my father, Oliver, Rey, Styx. And, not least, me and what I have become. Round and round they swirl, always accompanied by that constant growling at the back of my skull. I can't come up with any answers, not on my own. But who is there to ask? The wolves, I guess.

We travel through a valley and the sun, already low in the sky, disappears behind a hill. Calin turns on the headlights as we begin the ascent through a densely wooded area.

"About ten more minutes," he says, offering me an encouraging smile. "You ready?"

"No," I say, then follow up with a question that I'm certain makes me sound like I'm about ten years old. "You're not going to leave me straight away, are you?"

His smile is so warm it momentarily displaces the horror of the last few days. It's hard to say what this connection between us is. I don't do close relationships, and this is definitely not the time to develop that type of feeling.

"I'll stay the night, if that's okay with them."

"However long you can manage," I say.

As we crest the hill and break out of the forest, we find ourselves looking down on a sea of lights.

"That's it?" I ask, surprised at the scene that stretches below us.

"That's it. That's the werewolf camp."

2

I think it's fair to say I'd made some assumptions about what kind of habitat a wolf pack would live in. An image had taken form in my mind. A few rickety, wooden cabins. Possibly a caravan or two. Washing lines strung between wooden poles. A bit like you see in old American films. But this expanse of lights, extending across the valley, indicates something vast. It's hard to tell in the darkening sky, but judging by the amount of illumination, there must be around a hundred buildings, maybe more. The site seems to have been well planned, not at all haphazard as I'd imagined a village populated by wolves would be. The track we're on winds down towards it.

"It's like one of those remote civilisations you see in documentaries. You know, the type where cults live."

"I'll take your word for it," Calin replies, matter-of-factly. "I'm not much of a documentary person."

I suspect his curt answer is a polite way of stopping my questioning, but now I've started, I can't stop.

"Why do you think they built it here, at the bottom of a valley? Surely, being at the top of the hill they'd be better able to protect themselves?"

"I don't think they've had to worry about protecting themselves in a long time. They're well-hidden here. And, with the dense forest surrounding them and this single access route, they have a good view of anyone approaching."

There's no denying that. We must have been in their line of sight for well over a mile. Now we're closer, I can see the buildings more clearly. While they do have a certain rustic look about them, they are far from rudimentary shacks. In fact, it feels rather like an exclusive, getaway resort.

Calin slows the car to a crawl and it rumbles over a cattle grid and past a large, metal gate. At last, we're no longer looking down at the village; we're in it.

"So, I guess my arrival here isn't exactly a secret." I observe.

I've no idea what I'd expected in terms of a welcoming party, but it certainly wasn't a hundred-odd people lining the edge of the road.

"I guess not. There's no need to be nervous though, trust me. Wait here, I'll go and find out what's going on."

As he stops the car, my eyes fall on a young boy standing just a few feet away, clutching his father's legs. Children. Of course, there are children here too.

A shudder rolls down my spine. As Calin reaches for the door handle, I grab his arm.

"Wait. The Council will be looking for me. If I'm here, I'm a risk to them, aren't I? To all of them."

He follows my line of sight to the small child, then slowly turns back around to face me.

"They know the situation. They don't believe there is a risk."

"So why do they look so scared?"

We look back outside, where hundreds of eyes are looking our way.

"I don't know, but I think it's because strangers are not something they're used to. Trust me, Narissa, this is your only choice."

He reaches for the door again, and this time I don't stop him. He opens it and steps outside.

Almost immediately, my skin starts to prickle and the hairs on my arms rise. A twitching has begun at the base of my neck and a small voice has started whispering in the back of my head. It's my own voice, but different. Deep and coarse. More resonant. I can't make out individual words, but I know exactly what it's saying: I need to transform. I must protect him. And myself. The twitching grows stronger and it's in my legs now, too. My wrists and fingers bend and start to claw.

"No!" I shout aloud, and the voice in my head immediately falls silent. My fingers soften just a fraction, although they are still quite rigid and bent. Great. It would appear I now have a split personality of some sort. But at least the other me seems to listen to the original one.

I look back out of the car. There are so many people

here that turning into a wolf could only make matters worse. If talking to myself helps keep things under control, then that's what I'll have to do.

Outside, Calin has his back to me, as a woman steps forward from the crowd. Strands of grey hair show from beneath her bandana, and she's dressed in ripped jeans and a vest top that wouldn't look out of place on someone a quarter of her age. I try to listen in, to read her lips even, but it's hopeless.

A moment passes, then another, and already it feels like he's been out there too long. After all, how much have they got to discuss? They were expecting me. Unless the gathering in numbers is to let me know they've changed their mind and make sure I leave. Maybe it's even worse than that. Perhaps this was just to lure me into a trap. It wouldn't be the first time that's happened. Again, there's that voice in the back of my mind, the wolf desperate to release itself. This time I don't need to shout to push it back down. I'm done waiting. But just as I reach for the door handle, Calin comes striding back towards me.

"You okay?"

"No," I say. "I feel like I'm gonna be sick."

"Well, please don't do it in my car. Do you have any idea how much it costs to get the seats cleaned?"

It takes me a moment to process what he has just said.

"Calin Sheridan, did you just crack a joke?"

He wrinkles his nose in mock disgust. "That sounds most unlike me."

"I know."

The humour lingers in his face for just a second before his expression changes to the serious one I'm used to.

"We need to go and see the Alpha."

"That doesn't sound good."

"Just a formality. She just wants to welcome you, that's all."

"She?" For some reason, I'd assumed the Alpha would be a man. I don't know if I'm more or less worried. "Okay, so where is she?"

With a nod of his chin, Calin gestures towards a row of houses that stretches out away from the road. "She's down there, apparently." He pauses. "You ready?"

"No," I say. "But let's go do this, anyway. Just remind me; how certain are you they won't kill me the moment I step out here?"

He glances briefly past me then offers a half-shrug.

"About sixty-forty."

"Which way?"

The twitch of his eyebrow is minuscule, but it's there.

"I think we should go now," he says.

Hoping the comment was a poorly executed attempt at another joke, I take a deep breath and step outside the car.

Thankfully, the crowd has dispersed, almost as if they were expecting someone else. Of the few remaining, several are children. Are they wolves? I wonder. Can you become a wolf that small? For a split second, my thoughts are distracted by the idea of tiny wolf cubs running around.

Calin takes my hand and squeezes it gently. "You're here now. The hardest part is done."

The woman with the bandana nods at us and, without speaking, leads us down a gravel path. Forcing back the fear, I take Calin's arm. The stones crunch beneath my feet and go a little way towards distracting me from the thought that any second now one or more wolves is going to jump us and rip Calin's head clean from his neck and then do the same to me, if not worse. Maybe it's just paranoia after falling for Styx's ambush, but I'm convinced that this whole thing is a trap. That we are walking into danger and, this time, there won't be anyone to swoop in and save me. The woman's voice brings me back to reality.

"Down there," she says, drawing to a halt and indicating a narrow path between two houses.

At first, I think she's got it wrong; from what I can see, there's nothing there apart from trees and more trees, and my fears of an ambush multiply as the prickling starts down my spine again. I'm just about to tell Calin as much, when a light glimmers in front of us A few metres in and a shape comes fully into view. It's a wooden cabin, but new and large too. Obviously, the Alpha would have the best of the best.

"I know you have questions," Calin says, as we approach the door. "But don't feel you have to ask everything all at once. You're going to be here a while. And you don't have to answer everything straight away, either."

Answer what? I want to ask. What can I possibly tell

them? Two days ago, I didn't even believe werewolves existed and now I am one. Besides, right now, the only thing I need to know is where I can find a bed to sleep in.

My heart's pounding. I take the steps up to the front door. I realise my whole body is trembling as I go to knock. My knuckles are only inches away when the door swings open. And, just like that, my whole world is turned upside down again.

3

"Narissa."

The voice instantly sends my inner wolf rampaging through my mind. No longer a whisper, it's roaring at me to set it free to attack the woman standing there. She is smiling so brightly, her eyes are practically glowing, or at least they would be if it wasn't for the shimmer of tears in them. Eyes that are the exact same shape as mine. And lips that curve in exactly the same way as the face I see in the mirror every day.

"Narissa, my baby girl." In a sweeping movement, she wraps her arms around me, engulfing me in her warmth and her scent. It's heady. Dizzying. Foreign and yet, at the same time, so familiar. Held in this women's embrace, my thoughts whirl. Images rise and swirl, all-consuming and addling. It's as if every memory from my childhood is rushing to the surface.

I see myself holding my parents' hands. Swinging between them as we navigate a cobbled pathway in the country village where I grew up, their laughter ringing in the air. The scene switches. They are laughing again, this time as we eat ice creams on a pebble beach. My mother is struggling to keep her hair from blowing into hers. My father holds it back so she can eat. Another switch, this time to a dining table and a family meal, with a place laid for a toy. A doll I had for years, now long forgotten.

"My darling, darling girl. You've grown so big!"

"No. No," I cry.

I twist away, stumbling back down the steps.

"Did you know about this?" I shout at Calin.

"Narissa ..."

"Did you know she was here? Did you know my mother was alive?"

The disbelief in his eyes is nearly a match for mine.

"Narissa, I ... no!"

"You swear to me?"

"He's telling you the truth, my darling. I have never set eyes on this vampire before today."

My shock now transforming into pure rage, I turn back to her. Her arms are still reaching out for me, but I swipe them away.

"Don't you dare speak to me like that," I hiss. "I don't even know who you are."

"Narissa, my— I'm sorry. It was safer this way."

"Safer?"

She presses her top lip with a knuckle of her index finger.

"Why don't you come inside? We can talk. I can answer all your questions."

"I'm not going anywhere with you."

The growling starts up again, but this time it's audible. I feel Calin flinch at my side, but this woman, my mother, doesn't so much as bat an eyelid.

Shaking, I spin around and march back the way we came.

"We're leaving."

"Narissa, please," she calls after me.

"Stay away from me!" I growl back at her.

Every muscle in my body, from my head to my toes, is taut and trembling. There's a heat burning beneath my skin as the wolf begs to be released to rip her limb from limb. But even with my heart torn out, I'm not stupid. If she's the Alpha, it means she must be strong. Certainly strong enough to beat a newly turned wolf like me.

"Calin. We're going."

At least he's got the sense not to argue with me.

Back at the car, I nearly rip the door off its hinges in my haste to get in. For no reason that makes sense, I take the driver's seat but, considering he's got the keys, I can't actually go anywhere. I content myself with hammering my fist down on the steering wheel. The blare of the horn startles a flock of starlings, which takes flight from a nearby tree. Sod it. Like I care about a bunch of birds.

"You swear you didn't know?" I snap, the moment he gets into the passenger seat. "You really didn't know she was here?"

"On your life."

"How could you not? I thought five-hundred-year-old vampires knew everything."

"To start with, I'm not five hundred, and secondly ..." His voice fades to a whisper. "I didn't have any idea. I'm so sorry. I can't imagine what a shock it must have been."

"No, you can't."

How could he? I still can't quite take it in. Over twenty years. That's how long it's been since I last saw her, and all this time, she's been here. My mother is alive. Not only that, but she's the Alpha of a wolf pack. Everything I've held true has been a lie.

"Do you want to talk about it?" Calin asks softly.

"No." I shake my head. I do not want to talk about it at all. But heat is building behind my eyes and my breathing is growing more and more laboured. I hear the words spilling from my tongue before I can stop them.

"Ten years. For ten years, I've thought I was an orphan, Calin. For ten years I've had no one. Until Oliver, until Rey ..." My voice catches in my throat. "I needed someone—anyone—to be there for me. And there wasn't. I was on my own. I was always on my own."

I think back to the years I spent in the foster-care system where I was a nonentity. Just a body to be passed around from one place to the next. After a while, I learned to not even bother unpacking my rucksack. I was never anywhere long enough to make it worth the effort. I suppose Jessop, the Head of Blackwatch, tried to be there for me, but he never believed I'd seen a vampire kill my father. Besides, he was the one who cleared out all my dad's belongings when he died, before I'd had a chance to save even a single shirt. How could I trust someone like that?

"I used to daydream …" I say out loud. "All the time. I'd drift into these reveries about how at least my parents were together again. Not like I even really believed in any of that stuff, you know. But that was the best I could come up with, that at least after my dad died, he got to be with her. But now, I find out that, all this time, she's been here. *She* was never alone, and she sure as hell never gave a shit about me."

"I'm sure that's not true," he replies.

I shake my head.

"Yeah," I snort. "Why raise your kid when you can be an all-powerful alpha?" With another sniff, I wipe away the tears and snot. "It doesn't matter, anyway. I don't know who that woman is. She's nothing to me. What I know is that I got by just fine without her up to this point and I'm not accepting any handouts now. Come on. We're leaving."

I stretch out my hand for the keys. He doesn't move. A dark shadow crosses his face.

"Okay, you drive," I say and turn to the door.

"I know you don't want to hear this, but you don't have a choice. I don't know if this is something you and your mother—"

"*Freya.* Do not call her my mother. She lost the right to that title when she played dead."

"I get it. I don't know if this is something you and she will ever be able to get over, but what I do know is that no vampires are going to waltz in here unannounced. But go

CHAPTER 3

anywhere else—literally, anywhere else—in the world, and they will hunt you down and kill you. This can't be about your mother. It has to be about you and what you have to do to survive. So, I know this is an almost impossible ask, but I need you, just for a moment, to forget about her. Forget about what she did and didn't do and who she is. Ask yourself one question: do you want the vampires to find you?"

My head is down. Dark, wet circles are blooming on the horrible jeans.

"Of course I don't."

"Good," he says, lifting his hand to my face and brushing away some of the tears. "Because I really don't want that, either. But, for now at least, it means we're stuck here."

"Calin, I can't. I can't do it."

His thumb is still against my cheek as he speaks.

"Narissa Knight, you can do anything."

"Not this, Calin. Not this."

"Really? You, who tracked down a vampire—a member of the Vampire Council, no less—and also managed to steal classified documents from a Blackwatch operative—"

"My friend—"

"From a Blackwatch operative, and who succeeded in fooling an incredibly intelligent vampire into thinking that you were a blood donor. Then infiltrated a vampire feeding cell—"

"And got another friend killed."

"Stop it. Stop doing that. I don't know everything, but

I know enough to tell you that you need to stop blaming yourself for things that were beyond your control. And that includes Rey's death."

I think it's the first time I've ever heard him say her name. And it hurts.

"Calin, you don't—"

"I know you didn't drag her in there, just as I know you wouldn't have stolen from Grey if you'd had any other choice. I know you would never put one of your friends in harm's way. Narissa, you stood up to a vampire that even his peers wouldn't have dared to oppose. You can do this. You've just got to want to. You've got to want to survive this."

It sounds so simple. But I'm so tired. So very tired of fighting. Of battling everything. Of feeling so damned weak. The tears continue to trickle down my cheeks.

"Of course I do," I say, eventually.

"Good, then stay here. I'll see to the rest." He takes my hands and squeezes them tightly. "You can do anything," he says, and I really wish I could believe him.

4

No matter how many angles I look at it from, all I can come back to is, *how?* How could she leave me out there in the world, knowing that this might happen? How could she condemn me to those foster homes, knowing what I could have become? Did she not know about Dad's work? She must have done. I knew vampires were real before I knew Father Christmas wasn't. Surely, she realised ...

"They've sorted out a place for you to stay." Calin is back sooner than I expected. "It's just a little way into the forest, apparently."

"I'm not staying here?" *With her?* is what I mean. I'm not sure if I'm relieved or not.

"No. They're going to take us there now."

He nods, gesturing through the car window. For a second, I'm afraid to look, just in case he's indicating her, Freya, but when I look out, it's the bandana lady and a young girl who are waiting for us. My mother is nowhere in sight. I guess that's her MO. Get other people to do her dirty work. Why break the habit of a lifetime?

The girl looks to be around seventeen and is smiling broadly. In fact, she looks almost excited. Great. Happy people. Just what I want.

"I'm not going anywhere," Calin says. "Not tonight. Not until you're ready."

"Thank you," I reply and exit the car.

"Narissa." Bandana woman steps forward, extending a hand. "It's a pleasure to meet you. I'm Chrissie. I'm sorry we've got a bit of a walk to your cabin, I'm afraid. Newly turned wolves aren't allowed to stay in the village."

"They're not?" For a place I'd assumed to be entirely inhabited by wolves, this seems a strange rule. The girl is quick to address my confusion, as we make our way towards the forest.

"Newly turned wolves aren't allowed in the village because of the control issue," she explains. "You are a newly turned wolf, right? I thought I heard someone say that."

"I guess—"

"Actually, nobody is allowed in the village in wolf form, full stop. You have to be human once you're this side of the boundary woods. But after you've undergone your ceremony, you're not allowed back here at all, until you're properly a gamma."

"Gamma."

"Officially part of the pack. Well, I suppose you could say we're all automatically that, but gamma's our first rank. We can't fight or stuff until we're a gamma, and don't get to be that until we can regulate the change."

She pauses for breath and I feel sure she's going to carry right on talking, but I manage to get a question in first.

"So why can't you be in the village until then?" I ask.

"Because of the children. They don't want us turning out of control and terrifying them. I used to think it was a stupid rule, too, before my ceremony. But it's so tricky, right? Controlling it? That was over a year ago, so I'm completely fine now, but one day in that first week, I transformed over two-hundred times. Honestly, two hundred! I counted. Wolf, human, wolf, human. Nonstop. That was a seriously bad day. I thought I'd never get the hang of it. Although I was sorted pretty quick. I got to be gamma after a couple of months. It should actually have been even sooner, but someone here is rather overprotective."

Chrissie smiles, a hint of embarrassment flashing in her eyes. "Please excuse Lou. She gets a little carried away."

Lou rolls her eyes.

"And please excuse my mother. As a beta, she sometimes forgets that not all of us manage to control our turning in the first week."

"Your mother. You're her ... daughter?"

Just saying the word causes a surge of pain and anger to wash over me. That's what a mother-daughter relationship is supposed to be like. Communication. Openness. Not pretending to be dead.

"You don't have any bags," Chrissie says, suddenly. "You don't have any clothes?"

"N ... no," I stutter, wondering where the sudden change of direction came from. "We had to leave rather swiftly."

"Of course you did." She turns to her daughter. "Lou, go and do a sweep around the village please. Find Narissa something to wear."

Lou's face falls. Clearly, she was looking forward to telling me everything she knows about the pack and being a wolf.

"She'll need everything, mind. Get some toiletries too. And plenty of snacks. I suspect these guys are starving."

"Won't there be food in the hut?" Lou offers a half objection.

"Maybe, but if there's not, you're going to have to head all the way back here again, and you know you can't carry things as a wolf. What do I always say?"

"Do a job once and do it properly. What about him? Do I need to get clothes for him, too?"

There's a hint of fear in her eyes when she looks at Calin, which doesn't diminish even though he smiles at her.

"A spare T-shirt would be great," he says.

With a quick nod, she turns around and sprints back the way we came.

We're on the edge of a field now, with the village behind us and a massive expanse of forest ahead. A short way off to the side, is what seems to be a well, although the whole thing is strewn with clothes. It looks like some weird shrine to bad fashion, but before I get a chance to ask, Chrissie is speaking again.

"I'm sorry, Narissa, I didn't consider what Lou coming with us would mean. We have a lot going on at the minute, so I didn't bother arguing with her when she said she wanted to join us. I didn't think about how it would appear to you. That was thoughtless and I apologise. Please forgive me."

"Honestly, it's fine," I reply, not sure what else I can say. She knows who I am then, that much is obvious. Shame Freya wasn't half as concerned about upsetting me.

Dusk is well and truly upon us, and the evening light is a wash of silvery grey, but it's enough for us to find our way. Given that we're now in the middle of a forest, it's far louder here than I'd have expected. Owls hoot above us, as our feet crunch on twigs and fallen leaves and there's a constant hum of insects: grasshoppers, cicadas or whatever you call them. It sounds like we're closer to the Mediterranean than the Orkney Islands.

"It's not much further," Chrissie says, offering me a fleeting smile. "It's the closest hut to the village. We can even hear you if you yell loud enough."

"Let's hope there's no need for that," Calin says, with no trace of humour. That's actually a relief. Uber-serious Calin is at least some form of normality in all this.

"We can go by ourselves, if you tell us the way," I say, trying to offer her a way out of what is clearly an uncomfortable situation. "I'm sure Calin would be able to find it easily enough."

I receive another half-smile in response.

"It wouldn't be safe for you to be out in the woods on your own. The others don't know your scent yet. And with a vampire too ... Don't worry, it's just up here."

Silence falls as I walk almost shoulder to shoulder with Chrissie across a wooden bridge over a small stream while Calin follows behind.

"I should apologise for the way we must have seemed on your arrival. We've had a couple of rough weeks lately."

"Why's that?" I ask, half out of curiosity, half because it seems the polite thing to do.

"It's a pack matter. I'm sure your mother will fill you in when you're ... integrated."

I snort and immediately regret it. Despite all the crappiness, I feel bad for Chrissie. She was just trying to make conversation, again.

After another five minutes of walking and we reach the cabin.

"They're not exactly luxurious," she says, pushing open the door and leading us in. "But there's a wood-burning stove to cook on, and the mattresses are as good as the ones in the village. There's no running water, I'm afraid, but there should be enough in those glass bottles on the shelf for now. We'll bring you more from the village in the morning."

I look around. Spartan is barely an adequate description. Apart from the mattresses, there's only one small

CHAPTER 4

wooden chair, a low chest of drawers—which must double as a table— and a fire. No toilet. No sink. It's a far cry from glamping.

"Thank you," I say. At this point, I really don't care. I just want to shut the door—any door—on the world and be done with it. I get the feeling that Chrissie senses that.

"Sorry about Lou," she says, again. "And I'm so sorry about Michael, too. I heard what happened."

The use of my father's name catches me by surprise. No one used to call him that in front of me.

"You heard what happened to him?" I repeat her words.

"Only on the grapevine."

"Oh."

I don't know what else to say. This discovery is another twist of the knife in my gut. If Chrissie knew he was dead my mother would have, too, and therefore did realise that I would end up in foster care.

"I didn't know him well," she continues. "But from what I saw of him, he was good a man."

"You met him?"

"Only that once. Only when he—" She stops short, shaking her head and muttering to herself like she's put her foot in it again. "I'm sorry, it's not my story to tell," she says, stepping outside. "If you need anything, we're not that far away." A second later she turns and disappears into the shadows, leaving me alone with a vampire, in a hut, in a wood.

"How are you feeling?" Calin asks. "Do you want to sit down? Lie down?"

I'm about to answer that I'm so tired I could sleep standing up, when I notice his own weariness and the dark rings under his eyes. Something I've not seen before. And that's when it hits me; I have no idea when he last fed.

5

Two weeks ago, the thought of being stuck alone in a ten-foot-by-ten-foot hut, with a member of the Vampire Council, would've been the stuff my nightmares were made of. But a lot can happen in fourteen days, and as I pace up and down the tiny floor, Calin currently looks far more terrified of me, than I feel of him.

"You need to rest. You should sleep," he says.

"You need to feed. When did you last eat?"

"I am fine, Narissa. I am not the one I'm worried about right now."

"You mean you're worried that if I get tired and emotional, I'll turn into a wolf."

I stop and glower at him, but he stares back at me with absolute confidence.

"No," he says. "I'm not worried about that."

"You're not?"

"I may have known you only a short time, Narissa

Knight, but nothing, including your own genetic makeup, is going to make you do something you don't want to."

He stands up from the chair he's taken in the corner, and for a minute I think he's going to say something more. But instead, he walks three paces across the room to where I am.

"What can I do?" he asks me. His eyes reflect orange from the sulphur yellow of the low-hanging bulb that lights our small space. "What do you need?"

What do I need? What a question. There are so many things. For a start, I need to be left alone with my own thoughts for just one minute, without this voice, this incessant gnawing at the back of my skull. Although that would probably drive me crazy, too, with so much to process. Freya. Dad. Oliver. Rey. Myself.

My breathing starts to hitch. I don't want to cry again. But I'm so exhausted from feeling this exhausted. As I try to force my emotions back down, Calin is suddenly close to me, wraps his arms tightly around me and pulls me into his chest. My immediate thought is to object, but then I realise I don't want to. *This* is what I need.

"I've got you," he says, "You're fine. I've got you."

As I relax against his chest, I try to remember the last time someone held me like this. Oliver. He used to hug me a lot. We'd be walking home from somewhere like the cinema and there'd be a chill in the air, and he'd yank me in so tight next to him that I'd struggle to walk straight, and we'd start laughing. Or we'd curl up on his sofa, watching some true crime series, sharing a family-size bag of mini eggs. Then, when Rey disappeared having been banished from Blackwatch, we would cuddle together wondering where she might be or what she might be doing. Wondering if she'd managed to find a coven, a new home. Only Rey's not missing anymore, she's dead, and I suspect Oliver would now rather run a mile than get near enough to hug me again.

The thought causes me to move even closer to Calin. Deeper into his skin. He's warmer than I'd imagined. Soft, malleable. Almost human. I stay there with my head against his chest. I want him to stay here and not just for tonight. I need him to help stop this whirring in my mind. It seems easier to keep the inner wolf in check with him around, and I'm about to say as much when a bang on the door destroys the moment.

"Clothes and food delivery!" Lou's voice announces. I break away from him very much aware that, before now, huggers had not been our relationship status.

"I think she might be one of those people with unlimited energy," I say, offering a small smile to ease the tension that we both seem to be feeling.

"I get that impression too. Maybe it'll rub off."

I laugh as I move to open the door. Despite the sudden interruption, I feel marginally better, like Calin holding me so tightly forced a few of my broken pieces back together again.

"I don't think anyone wants to know what I'd be like with a constant source of energy," I reply and open the door.

"Great, you're still up," Lou grins, her arms laden with

bags. "I was worried you might have fallen asleep already. Transition's tiring, right? One boy slept for the entire first two weeks after his ceremony. I'm serious. He ended up way behind the rest of us, with the whole blocking stuff and everything, but I get it. It can be so draining. Bones breaking. Bones healing. You must be zonked. Anyway, I managed to get you guys a few bits and pieces. I'm pretty sure there should be stuff in here you can use."

Her sentences roll into one, but I notice the mention of this ceremony again. That appears to be when they change into a wolf for the first time, although my focus doesn't stay on that for long. A few bits and pieces is a massive understatement. In the short time we've been here, she's managed to round up two huge bags of clothes. By the looks of things, there's more in them than my wardrobe back in London.

"Is that all for me?" I ask.

"And him," she gestures towards Calin. "Sorry it took me so long. I'd have been quicker as a wolf, but you know—no hands."

Although she's speaking to me, her eyes keep flickering back and forth to Calin, a wary distrust evident. She lowers her voice just a fraction.

"I can stay here with you, if you want. You know, for … company?"

She's not exactly subtle, but it's kind. A sweet offer to try and protect me, I suppose. Although, if she thinks whispering's going to stop a vampire hearing what she's saying, she's got a lot to learn.

"Calin's fine. Let's just say I trust him a lot more than anyone else in the village."

A look of hurt flashes across her face and I realise she thinks the dig was at her and the rest of the pack, rather than who I had intended it for—Freya. The slightest twinge of guilt flickers within me, but I squash it down fast. After all, it's not like I have good reason to trust any of them yet. And not to play tit-for-tat, but she did start it with the whole not trusting Calin issue.

"Is that everything?" I ask, refocusing attention back to the bags.

She shakes her head. "There are some extra pillows and things outside. Some of the others like sleeping as wolves. Me, I prefer being human, even out here. And I can never have too many pillows. Didn't know if you were the same. There's food too. Snacks. Human snacks, obviously. I know you could change and go hunting if you want to, but it's weird, right? Getting your head around eating rabbits and things? I mean, I've been a wolf for a year now and I still hate eating as one. Give me a proper roast dinner any day."

There's finally a pause in her unending stream of comments.

"Thank you. That's really thoughtful, isn't it, Calin?" I say, trying to draw him into the conversation, in the hope she'll start to see that he's not going to go all killer vampire on us. "Calin? Lou's brought clothes and food and pillows. Did you hear?"

His head is cocked to the side and his forehead is

wrinkled in concentration. He doesn't blink. It's like he's focusing on something else, something far away.

"Calin, what is it?"

"Does he do that often?" Lou hisses in my ear.

"No," I say, my eyes still locked on him. I've not heard of vampires turning pale before, but if it's possible, I'd say he's pretty close to it. I wait another moment then, just as I start to move towards him, he suddenly snaps out of it.

"Something doesn't feel right," he says, finally acknowledging us. "Something definitely isn't right."

He moves past me to the door, where Lou has the sense to step to the side and allow him through. Night has fallen and it's almost pitch-black outside, yet I can feel a change, too. Like the hush before a storm. And the moment I think this—that's when it starts.

6

At first, it's a single scream. Ear piercing and agonised, it cuts through the dark.

"What was that? Was that a person?" I ask, but before anyone can reply, a huge wailing starts up and the anguish and pain are so raw, they strip the breath right out of my lungs.

"I have to go," Lou says, spinning back away from us.

"Wait! What ...?" I start to say but too late. Already a blur of red-brown fur, she is bounding back to the village the quickest way she knows how. As a wolf.

"Stay here," Calin says, briefly resting a hand on my shoulder. "Shut the door and don't open it for anyone except me or Freya."

"Why? What's going on?"

"I don't know. Just stay here."

"Calin ...?" I begin, only to realise I'm already alone.

"Seriously?" I complain into the darkness.

I start to close the door, only to stop and stare down

the path. I'm torn. The wails have faded and there have been no more ear-splitting shrieks like that first one, but the effect still lingers, like a cloud shrouding the forest. Something has happened in the village. Something bad. And I'm here. Away from it but with only a wooden hut to protect me, and I'm pretty sure it doesn't even have a lock on it.

Besides, there's Calin to think of, too. Those wolves didn't seem thrilled to see us and I can't risk anything happening to him. My friends have a habit of putting themselves in danger and I'd rather not make it three for three. That leaves me no option but to follow him.

There's just one major problem. Other than by moonlight out in the open, how will I find my way? The forest is so dense I'll barely be able to see my hand in front of my face. My human senses aren't going to cut it. I need to be a wolf.

The thought is all it takes. At that very instant, the growling inside my head crescendos to a full-on roar. Then the pain starts. First one bone snaps, then another, then the cracking reverberates down my spine and through my skull. The muscles tear and reform in a thousand different ways. I howl in pain, although it's fleeting this time and, in less than a heartbeat, I'm standing on all four paws in wolf form and with my clothes in shreds around me. Panting, I move one paw, then another, as if my mind is the puppeteer of the body I'm now inhabiting.

Lifting my head, I sniff the air, amazed at how clear everything comes through. The damp of the earth hits me first, but then all the other odours sweep in. The rotting oak leaves that litter the forest floor, a rabbit warren, dug into the earth somewhere nearby and then, amongst it all, fresh and strong, Calin and Lou's scents.

Time to see how well this nose works, I say to myself.

It's all so natural. Letting my instincts take over, I speed through the undergrowth, clearing fallen trees and branches, barely grazing the grass beneath my feet as I follow the exact same path that Chrissie, Lou and Calin took. I'm not perfect. When the stream appears, and I leap to cross it instead of using the bridge, my feet land on a patch of silty earth and I start to slip back towards the water but immediately correct myself.

It's not just the smells that are clearer now, my sight and hearing can pick up everything from the panicked dash of a mouse to the rustle of an owl's wings. In a fraction of the time it took us to reach the hut on human foot, I'm standing at the edge of the forest. While Calin's scent is still strong, Lou's has all but disappeared. That's when I remember her words: no wolves in the village.

A guttural growl comes from my canine throat. After so long itching to be released, the wolf in me has no desire to be caged again, but I can't mess this up. Whatever's going on, I need to stick to the rules.

I need to go into the village, I say to myself. Another growl escapes my now drooling lips. *I need to go into that village, and I need to be human.*

My hackles rise, as my wolf body defends itself against my own mind. I immediately block every wolf-like thought and sensation that's rolling through me, from the feel of the wind in my fur to the scent of the earth and grass. But I'm not changing back! Shit! Now I know what Lou was talking about. Typical. Becoming the wolf is easy. Turning back to my natural-born, human state is the problem.

I need to be a human, I say to myself again only, this time, I visualise what it's like to be human. I imagine my two feet standing on the earth. Fingers, toes, ears that aren't covered in fur. Still nothing. Okay, what do I like most about being human? Eating? That's got to be high up on the list. Wolves eat meat, so no point in thinking about that, then. Try something else. Like mashed potato. Dark chocolate. Diet Coke. Something shifts inside me. There's a clicking in my spine. Diet Coke! I force myself to remember the sweetness of it. The fizz on my tongue as I swallow one mouthful, then another. How about Margherita pizza? The cheese oozing over a deep-pan crust. God, I would love a pizza right now. Garlic bread. Dough balls. The whole shebang. Now it's my stomach growling as I think about all the toppings I'm going to order on my next pizza—if I ever get out of this place to have one. That's when I realise. My stomach's growling. Mine, not the wolf's. By the time I've shaken my head clear, I'm standing upright on my two, furless feet.

"I'm human!" I say, this time out loud with my actual voice. "Human and, yet again, naked."

I'm back where we entered the forest, just a few feet from the strange, clothes-covered well that doesn't seem odd at all anymore. Actually, it's a really clever idea. Assuming it is more than a coincidence—and that there are no rules on what you can and can't take—I walk over and grab the first thing off the top: a long, plaid shirt with half the buttons missing. It covers half-way down my thighs, showing far more flesh than I'm used to, but it'll do. I don't have the time to hunt through to see if there's anything better.

Trying to do up the remaining fastenings, I start to sprint back towards the road.

Whatever fitness I acquire as a wolf, it clearly doesn't transfer to the human me. Almost immediately, I'm out of breath, and my progress is hindered even more by the fact that I'm barefoot. Every step feels like I'm walking on hot coals, but I keep going, spurred on by the sounds. The wailing has been replaced by weeping and hollow sobbing.

When I reach the road, I slow down. People are running back and forth; parents are ushering children back into the houses. Others are comforting each other as they weep, barely able to keep themselves upright. As respectfully as I can, I push my way through the crowd, to find Freya standing on the bed of a large pickup truck, a body lying at her feet.

"Move out of the way!" she's shouting. "Make room! We need to get her to the medical centre right now! Find Gregory! Esther, grab hold of her feet! Gently!"

Over the last twenty-four hours, I've seen a lot of bodies, mainly in the form of dead vampires. (And to be fair, I was the one responsible for killing many of them.) But, for most of it, I was a wolf. There was a mental and physical barrier between what I was doing and seeing and my human mind. But there's no such protection now, and I find myself walking towards the scene—is mesmerised the right word? No—confused by the sight of the corpse.

It's a human. Adult, judging by the size, but that's where my comprehension ends. There's so much damage, so much bruising and swelling, that I can't tell if it's male or female, young or old. The hair is matted,and one hand is dangling by a tendon, the fingers twisted at unnatural angles and the knuckles bloody. Bile rises in my throat, and nausea and dizziness sweep in, sending my head spinning.

"Narissa, what are you doing here? You shouldn't be in the village."

It doesn't even register that it's Freya talking to me. A short while ago, seeing her alive had been enough to make me want to launch the wolf at her. Now, that seems of little concern.

"What happened to them?"

A small whimper comes from the body. I hadn't considered the person could still be alive. I don't know if that makes it better or worse. Surely someone can't survive in that state for long. Two people jump up to their aid, one with water, the other with a towel.

"Move out of the way!"

Someone pushes me to the side before also leaping on the back of the truck. A moment later, a group of people sweep in with a makeshift stretcher, removing the body under my mother's supervision.

"We need to find out what could do this. We need to

know why she's not transforming to heal. I need answers people. What's going on?"

As Freya jumps down, I freeze. Part of me wants to help. Not her specifically but these people who are in such pain. But I can't do anything except step back and let her pass.

I'm about to start my hunt for Calin, when a voice calls out from the dark, clear and sharp even amongst the noise of the crowd.

"Freya!"

It stops her in her tracks and me too, for that matter. She blinks before shaking her head.

"Calin. Whatever you want, I don't have the time right now. In case you can't see, I have a bit of an issue going on here."

"You need to tell me what's happening."

"I don't need to tell you anything, vampire."

He dips his head. "I apologise. That came out wrong. Please, I would appreciate it if you would tell me what has happened here. I may be able to help."

Her jaw clicks from side to side as she considers whether it's worth the effort of replying to him. She decides it is.

"We don't know what's going on. That's the truth of the matter. Not that it's any of your business, but six members of my pack went missing. We found this one, very badly injured, and she's not healing. I have no idea what could have done this."

"I do," he replies. "It was a vampire. A vampire did this."

Her mouth twists and she shakes her head again. "Look, I know you found a rogue up here recently, but it can't be that again. There's no blood drainage, to start with. Besides, such an attack wouldn't explain why she's not healing or why she didn't turn to protect herself. Now, if you don't mind—"

"Freya."

I've never heard so much power and strength in his voice before. It makes the hairs on my arms bristle. Every pair of eyes is on him. His remain fixed on my mother.

"I mean no disrespect to you or to your pack, but believe me, we need to talk. Now."

7

She doesn't want me here right now, she's made that clear enough, but Calin was blunt.

"Everything to do with vampires and wolves effects Narissa now, too. We might as well save ourselves the time and let her sit with us."

While still unimpressed by my presence, Freya didn't put up any more objections. So now it's me, Calin, her and Chrissie, sitting in a small room. We headed into the first building nearest the road, which looks to be some kind of all-purpose storeroom-cum-pub-cum-office. There's a desk on one side but also a bar and a whole ton of boxes. There's proper lighting though, not like in the hut.

At this precise moment, no one is talking. As we came here, the woman was being carried into a nearby building. That's obviously where the Beta would prefer to be, not here. Chrissie's eyes go constantly to the window, checking. Waiting to see if anyone appears outside with news. It could only be bad news, I guess. She couldn't possibly expect good news this quickly. By contrast, Freya's attention is solely on Calin.

"You've got five minutes. I want to know how it would be possible for a vampire to beat someone to within inches of their life and then not drink a sip of their blood. Not to mention how they'd be able to stop them turning into a wolf to defend themselves in the first place or after the attack to improve their chances of healing. When she was found, she managed to say a few words. She'd obviously had enough strength to get away from whoever was holding her, so she should have had more than enough strength to transform. It just doesn't make sense."

Increased healing rates, I think to myself. Good to know, although not something to dwell on at this moment. Instead, what I'm thinking is where would Calin be right now, if I'd not taken that girl's place as a blood donor and walked into his flat that night. My life has been turned upside down in the last few weeks, but I've done a pretty good job of messing his up, too.

"You know that werewolves were first created by vampires, to be an invincible army to fight to the death for them," he starts.

"Please don't tell me you're about to mansplain our own history to us, Calin." Freya snaps back.

Despite myself, the corner of my mouth twitches.

"Apologies, that was not my intention, I just need to check we're on the same page. As you know, the wolves were not quite so, shall we say, receptive to this idea."

"What you mean is that a werewolf is not designed for domestication."

"That's one way of putting it, yes. I know the general belief is that once the vampires discovered the wolves were not going to do their bidding, they aimed to eradicate them entirely, and at times they did come close to this, but I suppose you are also aware that there have been several attempts, through the centuries to try to return them to their intended function."

"They will never succeed."

"I accept that, as do most of my kind. But some believe that even if they can't control wolves, there are other uses for them."

"Other uses?" I find myself asking, and Calin glances at me briefly before nodding and continuing.

"Just after the war, I heard about an incident. An anti-Blood Pact vampire had caught a lone wolf and was using it for training."

"Training?"

"Fight training. There is little else on the planet that gives a vampire a real challenge. Even in human form a werewolf can withstand far more punishment than any normal man could and with the bonus of rapid healing, too."

This sounds pretty logical to me. One super-strong, supernatural being sparring with another super-strong, supernatural being. I guess a regular CrossFit gym doesn't cut it if you're two hundred years old and immortal. Chrissie and Freya are shaking their heads.

"What has that got to do with this?" Freya asks.

"Alena is in human form. If she had come into contact with a vampire and they had tried anything, she would have turned, transformed to protect herself."

"Unless she couldn't."

My mother snorts. "Alena's ceremony was over ten years ago. There's nothing in the world that could have stopped her from transforming if she wanted to."

"That's not strictly true. A witch could do that."

The temperature in the room seems to plummet.

"A witch?" Freya's eyebrows arch in that eerily familiar way. "Now I know you're wasting my time. No witch would ever make themselves known to a vampire, let alone help one of them torture one of my kind."

"Ordinarily, I would agree with you. But I saw this once before, nearly a hundred years ago. Besides, things here are not normal. You have half a dozen pack members missing. I take it this is not a regular occurrence."

"No." She speaks through gritted teeth. "It is not."

"And you said yourself, Alena should be healing by now, even in her human form. If I'm correct, then whatever hex or potion the witch has used on her not only stopped her transforming but also slowed the healing process."

"But why? What would be the point? A moment ago, you said it was the fast healing that made us wolves a perfect plaything for the vampires. Now you are saying the opposite. Why would they not want her to heal?"

"Because they're sick, sadistic bastards."

CHAPTER 7

Once again, it's me speaking, and there's a very clear image in my head. Styx. He said it himself—he wanted to watch me suffer. He wanted to enjoy the pain he was about to inflict. And he would have succeeded, too, had his venom not produced another, unforeseen effect on me.

Calin nods sadly in agreement.

"In the incident I spoke of, the pair—this witch and vampire alliance—they had kept the wolf captive for years. Torturing him, then letting him heal only to start the torment all over again."

There a moment's silence.

"And you think they could be doing that to the missing members of my pack?"

"I think it's not beyond the realms of possibility."

Inhaling slowly, Freya considers this.

"What you are saying—vampires torturing werewolves with the help of witches—it goes against all logic. Not to mention against the Blood Pact. If this is truly the case, it could have catastrophic effects. But you must have more evidence than just this one incident from a century ago."

This is a statement, not a question, yet she is obviously expecting an answer. We all are.

Calin nods his head slowly, "Yes, I do." He takes a moment before continuing. "As you know, I was sent up to this area a couple of weeks ago to deal with a rogue vampire. That is when I met you, Chrissie."

"I know all this," Freya replies.

"But I don't," I cut in. I don't mean to sound petulant, but it feels like there's a bit of background information I'm missing here. "Can you fill me in?"

I turn to Chrissie, but before responding, the Beta looks to Freya. While the Alpha doesn't look happy about this side-track in our conversation, she signals her approval.

"When I met Calin, it had been over two weeks since the first three members of the pack disappeared, and I was desperate to find any trace of them. They had gone to town together to run a few errands. Nothing out of the ordinary and well within the territory agreed with vampires decades ago. We go on almost weekly excursions, picking up supplies, gear for repairs, that type of thing. Sometimes, members stay away for a day or two, particularly when they're waiting for a delivery, but their extended absence was causing more and more concern. Two days had turned into a week. Then three more went missing. That was when we really started to worry. So, I went into town to try to find some clues. After visiting all their normal haunts and coming up empty, I dropped in on some of the more disreputable establishments. Not that I expected to find them there, but I wanted to make sure I'd left no stone unturned. That's when I spotted Calin, behaving—shall we say—suspiciously."

"I was trying to be discreet," he says, before taking up the story. "I had traced the scent of a vampire to this grubby little pub, not far from the cathedral. The problem was, it was full of people, which meant it was going to be a waiting game. I couldn't make my move in public, but the longer I waited, the more risk there was of her spotting me and fleeing. To be brief, when she finally got up to move—I believe following a young couple out—and I went after her, Chrissie accosted me."

"Did you know he was a vampire?" I ask her. "Could you smell him, even though you were in human form?"

"No." She shakes her head. "But I could tell."

"How?"

A small smile twists at the corner of her mouth. "He didn't blink."

"What?"

"He didn't blink. Vampires don't blink. Or rather they don't need to. There's not that constant reflex action going on."

"I will admit that I normally pay a little more attention to things like that," Calin concedes, "but I was too focused on getting the damned rogue."

"So, what happened then?" I ask. It could almost be the punchline to a joke: a vampire, a rogue and a werewolf walk into a pub …

"Chrissie pulled me aside and accused me of being what I am. I cursed myself for not having picked up on the wolf scent earlier. And then, because I couldn't see any other way out of it, I told her the truth. That if she didn't let me go right then, innocent people were going to get killed."

"That's it?" I say, mildly disappointed. I was expecting at least a small brawl ensuing.

"I knew he was telling the truth. I don't know how. I just did. Next thing, he's away in a flash, and I'm racing after him, hoping to find out if he has some idea what's happened to our pack members. When I finally catch up with him, he's standing over the body of the rogue, the heart ripped clean out of its chest."

I involuntarily jerk. Ripping a heart out is not something I can imagine Calin doing, and while I'm well aware that he's a vampire and vampires can do horrible things, this act is so violent, so blood thirsty, I just can't envision it. A lump forms in my throat as I realise that I actually don't know much about him at all.

"I still don't get what this has to do with our missing members and why you think it would involve witches," Freya comments. "Not to sound rude, but I have far more important things to deal with right now than listen to you talk about your heroics, killing a rogue vampire."

Our eyes turn back to Calin, but his are locked on the Alpha, as he bites his lip.

"That's the thing," he says. "I didn't."

"Didn't want."

"I didn't kill the rogue."

"But you just said—"

"She ripped her own heart out. She killed herself."

8

It's fair to say that Calin's confession leaves us all in a stunned silence. Ripping your own heart out? I guess if you've got a vampire's strength it would be physically possible, but how could someone, anyone, have the mental capacity to do that? It feels completely implausible.

"Say that again." Freya's interest is now piqued. "She ripped her own heart out? Why would she do that?"

Calin takes a deep breath.

"She was terrified. Terrified at having been caught. Terrified at the sight of me."

My mother offers a nonchalant shrug.

"Surely that can't be unusual? The last thing a rogue vampire wants is to get caught by a member of the Council. You are a member, are you not? That was why you were sent after them?"

"Yes, I am. But rogues are only scared of the Council if they know they're rogue in the first place."

"What does that mean?" I ask. I know I'm setting myself up here for another mythology lesson, but this time I get the impression I'm not the only one who needs it. His logic seems to be letting him down a little now.

"There are two types of rogue vampire," he says, his voice back in teaching mode. "Mostly, there are those who refuse to adhere to the Blood Pact, who want to continue in their old ways of debauchery and bloodlust and have no intention of ever forming any allegiance with humans. Obviously, because the Blood Pact has been in operation for so long, these are old vampires. Even older than me, often by a long way, which is how they manage to stay undetected for so long. They have hoarded money for centuries. Enough to buy private transport and bolt holes across the globe. How many there actually are, is anyone's guess. Some estimate there can only be a dozen or so, after the Vampire Council's success in dealing with them over the last century. Some feel there are many more."

"So that's the first type of rogue. What's the second?"

"The second is the one that we most frequently catch. The newly turned."

"Turned by who?" I query. "Surely that's illegal now, too?"

"By the first type of rogue. No vampire who has agreed to the Blood Pact is even capable of turning a human."

That's news to me.

"Why?" starts to form on the tip of my tongue, but I realise that's just going to take us further away from the point. Not to mention I seem to be the one asking all the questions. I press my lips together and wait for someone else to take up the mantle, which Chrissie quickly does. While she doesn't ask what I wanted to know, her question is probably more useful right now.

"So, why are these newly turned ones less fearful of getting caught? Why are they not concerned about the Vampire Council?" she asks.

"Because most of the time, they don't even know we exist. Of the hundred or so newly turned vampires I've caught over the last fifty years, only one has been over six months old."

"What? Why?"

"Because they don't know how to survive. They don't know how to feed without killing, or how to fight the urge for blood so that they can control themselves long enough to avoid getting caught. Without a mentor or guide, their first kill is usually enough to draw attention to them. They have probably only been turned for someone's amusement. An after-dinner plaything, perhaps. Most of them are abandoned by their sires before they even taken their first sip of blood. They certainly don't keep them around long enough to tell them about a secret organisation that requires them to only drink from obliging, donating humans. I'm usually the first of their kind they've ever seen, after their creator."

There's a sadness in his eyes as he speaks. Clearly, going out and dealing with rogues isn't as straightforward for Calin as a quick stake through the heart. He sees them for what they are. Creatures who were once human, who have been broken and abandoned. There's a strange similarity there to someone else, but I don't want to think too closely about that.

"So, this rogue who ripped out her own heart was an old one. That's why she was scared of you," I check.

"No. From the smell of her, she couldn't have been changed for more than a couple of weeks. But she had fed well in that time. I could detect the trace of over a dozen humans on her breath. That's far more than the number of deaths we'd had reported to us."

Chrissie and Freya look towards each other in alarm.

"But the moment she saw me, fear clouded her eyes. Before I'd even said a word to her, she plunged her hand into her chest. It was as if she was terrified of speaking with me. In all my time doing this, I have only had two others take their lives when I've caught up with them. And never like that. Never in such a gruesome way. And both were old vampires. I thought … well, I don't really know what I thought. Job done I suppose. The effect was the same. That was what mattered."

We wait. Expecting more. But he hasn't got anything else. His mind seems far away, and I'd bet a fair ton of money it's not a pleasant place to be. The rest of us have fallen into an uneasy silence. From somewhere outside comes a long, lone, wolf howl. A cry of pain and sadness.

"What does this mean?" Freya asks finally. "Why do you think it's linked to Alena and the other missing wolves?"

"Because both occurrences are such rarities. You know there has to be something untoward happening to your wolves and I know someone has taught a new vampire to be afraid of people like me. And they have happened so close to each other in time and place. I don't believe this is a coincidence. Do you?"

It's the first question he's asked all evening, and it's directed to Freya.

"Co-incidence or not, how can we be sure that this is a witch's doing?" she replies.

"It has to be," Calin says. "There's no other way that I can think of to stop a wolf from turning. Can you?"

"No."

"Then time will tell. I don't know much about spells and such, but a common-sense guess would lead me to believe that the fact that Alena is trapped in human form will be because of some kind of potion. Something within her system. All we can do is wait and hope it passes."

"Let's hope you are right," my mother agrees. "If she can just transform, the healing process will be much quicker. As a human, the pain …" Her eyes drift and I get the feeling she understands more about that than she wants to let on. With a shake of her head, the moment is gone, and she pushes back from the table to stand.

"Thank you, Calin. For now, as you say, all we can do is wait. However, I would like to think that, should we need your further help, we would have it?"

"Of course. And if Alena can make a good recovery, as we hope, then we will have more than just speculation to work on."

As Chrissie starts to bid us all goodnight, there is a short, hard rap on the door.

"Come in," Freya calls.

It opens, and a figure appears. No words leave his lips. He stands there, silently, for a moment, then bows his head, and I realise why he's not speaking.

"Alena is dead," I whisper.

9

No one speaks as Freya and Chrissie sweep out of the room, leaving Calin and me alone.

So that's it. She died. I wonder how much determination it took to last that long in such a horrific state. Maybe she was holding on to get back home and see her friends and family one last time. Outside, the sound of crying has begun again. Alena. That doesn't sound like the name of an old person. Freya said it had been over ten years since her ceremony. What would that make her? Based on Lou's age and how long since she was turned, she would probably be in her late twenties, though I'm not even sure it matters. She was obviously well loved. She was family.

"We should go back to the cabin," I say to Calin, when I find my voice again. "We should give them their space. Do you know the way?"

"I'll find it easily enough."

That's his modest way of saying yes.

We head straight outside. It's even harder out here, with people standing outside their homes, hugging one another as they weep. Some are kneeling on the ground, their heads buried in their hands. It's a close-knit community; that much is obvious.

Without making eye contact with anyone, I move as quickly as I can without running. The last thing these poor people need here is me, with all the danger I risk creating. I remember what it's like to lose someone you love. I've still got the scars. They never heal. You just learn to tolerate them.

As we leave the village, my thoughts drift to Dad. Did he know what she was? That she was still alive? I shake the second possibility away immediately. He would never have kept that from me. Never. And I'm not going to let Freya's deceit tarnish my memories of him. I've already got enough on my plate. With these thoughts comes that familiar inner-wolf itch again. Not helped by the sight of the forest boundary. Obviously, out there's where it feels it belongs.

"Chrissie said it wasn't safe for us out here without her," I remember, staring into the darkness that lies before us. "Not until all the wolves are used to our scent."

"It's not that far," Calin replies after a moment's contemplation. "I think most of them will have headed back to the village when the girl returned. I'll hear if anything is coming. Hold my hand. If we move swiftly, we'll get there soon enough."

A couple of weeks ago, I'd have refused to believe a single word from a vampire's lips, especially if it concerned my safety, but now I don't think twice as I slip my hand into his and let him lead me into the forest. Just a few short paces in and the lights from the village are entirely obscured by the foliage. It's easy to see how people get lost somewhere like this. It's shadows on top of shadows. Calin's pace is fast and part of me wants to tell him to slow down. The other part of me just wants to get back inside the hut as soon as freaking possible.

My pulse is drumming, and my ears are pricked for any sounds. Every bough creak, every chittering noise or snap of a twig, and I find myself jumping. It's ridiculous being scared like this, but I haven't come this far to be brought down by a member of my mother's pack, just a few feet from safety. I may have found out who killed my father, but I've got a whole heap more questions I need answering now.

Fortunately, after just a few more minutes, the rectangular shape of the cabin comes into view.

Swinging open the door, I switch on the light.

The cabin feels claustrophobic, like it's shrunk while we've been away. Not to mention at least ten degrees colder than before. I immediately start sifting through the bags Lou brought and pull out a jumper and pair of trousers.

"Do you want me to light the fire?" Calin asks.

"It's fine. I'll do it. Just give me a minute."

It doesn't take me long to find a jacket, and as soon as it's all on, I move to the wood burner, where a small box of matches sits, and start loading it up with firewood from a large basket. All the while, Calin is watching me, and for some reason I start to feel nervous.

"Actually," I say, "this wood seems a bit damp. It'll smoke too much. And we could do with some small twigs and dried leaves, that kind of thing, too."

"You really do know how to start a fire."

"It's not that hard."

I like Calin, I do, but I have no intention of sharing with him how my dad taught me on one of the camping trips we would go on. How we would toast marshmallows as the flames spat and danced and we'd laugh and make up ghost stories together. Those memories are precious. And private.

Without so much as a nod, he disappears through the door, to return almost immediately with an arm full of kindling.

"You could have at least tried to make it look like it took you a while," I say, unable to hide a hint of disappointment in my voice. To be fair, everything he's brought is dry. Thank goodness. I'm starting to see my breath in the cold air.

Five minutes later, there's a roaring fire and I'm back digging through the bags again, this time in search of food. Opening the first plastic box I come across, I find half-a-dozen cheese rolls. It's not fine dining, but it's filling, and it'll do just fine.

Calin is sitting in the chair, his eyes lost in thought.

"Shit," I say, putting the tub down again. "You haven't eaten either."

He looks at me and smiles. "It's all right. I'm okay."

CHAPTER 9

"You can't be. When did you last eat?"

"Really. It's not a problem. Don't worry about it. I'll go hunting later. Find a rabbit or something."

"Will that do?"

I can't imagine there's much blood in a rabbit, and no matter how much he tries to say otherwise, he's got to be hungry. I know vampires can go a fair while without food, but fighting all those other vamps to get me out of the dungeon must have used up a fair bit of energy, and it's not like he's had any time to rest since. Surely, some of my blood would be far better than whatever he could catch out there. But then again … I try to dismiss the thought, but now it's formed, I can't shake it.

"Narissa?"

"Is it because I'm a wolf?" I ask.

"What?" He sits up straight.

"Is that why you don't want to feed from me now? Because I'm …"

In a split second, he's standing in front of me, his face crumpled. He towers over me, and I'm not sure if this is meant to be intimidating or comforting. Either way, I don't move. Instead, I repeat my question.

"So, is it that? Do you not feed from wolves? Is my blood suddenly unappetising?"

"No, of course not."

"Then why won't you feed from me? What's changed?"

"What's changed?" His eyebrows rise. "Narissa, you have been through so much these last few days. Rey, Styx,

Oliver, your mother. The last thing you need is pressure from me."

"It's not pressure. I'm offering, Calin. Without you, I would be in a dungeon for the rest of my life, if not dead."

"Narissa, when I fed from you before, we had an arrangement. At least, I thought we did. But now … you don't have to feel obliged."

"You think I feel obliged?"

"Well, don't you?"

My mouth contorts as I prepare to object, but I stop myself and think about it.

He's saved me. More than once, now. He needs blood and I can give him that. But it's something more. As bizarre as it sounds, the thought of him feeding from me feels normal. He only did it twice, once when he barely took anything and a second time when he took so much I blacked out. But even that doesn't concern me. The idea of Calin's fangs piercing my skin is nothing compared to what I've been through since then. It's almost as if it could take me back to before this all got so damned screwed up.

"I feel like it might actually help me," I say, honestly.

It's clear from his expression that he doesn't understand, but that's okay. I don't need him to. All I need is for him to agree.

"All right," he says.

In terms of where, the only option in this little hut is for us to use the mattress. Without waiting for him to change his mind, I walk over and sit down, or rather plonk down in a rather unladylike way—a mattress on the ground is substantially lower than a bed—but I don't care.

"Just take what you need," I say, rolling up my sleeve.

"Are you sure? I can feed without using you," he says.

This time I don't bother to reply. I just wait for him to come and join me, which he does, somehow managing to lower himself down in an entirely dignified manner, just a few inches from me.

Nerves bubble through me. Not like before, though. I'm not worried if it will hurt, or whether he'll go too far. It's me I'm unsure about me. Whether the taste will be different after what I've become.

He lifts his hand, extending his index finger and the nail lengthens. As with all vampires, there's venom beneath it that acts as a mild anaesthetic. Or, if you happen to have a dormant werewolf gene lurking in your DNA, causes it to activate and you to transform into a four-legged, savage beast. Without the scratch that Styx inflicted on me, I would never have known what I really am.

"Do you want me to …?"

I shake my head. "No. I somehow think that after having survived my bones rearranging repeatedly, this'll be fine."

He offers a small smile, then reaches out his hand for my arm. My pulse is hammering as his fangs flick down. A second later, they plunge deep into me.

Immediately, the noise of my inner wolf, which has been my almost constant companion, disappears into oblivion. This is what I needed. For the first time since my first transformation, my mind is calm. All I'm aware of is the suction of his cold lips on my skin.

Just as I'm relaxing in the moment, he withdraws. The pain starts to diminish, and I can already feel the growl returning.

"Wait. You don't have to stop now. Please, take more."

"Narissa—"

I reach my hand up to pull his head back down towards me, but he's already on his feet. He's not looking at me but towards the door, which opens to reveal a figure standing there.

"Narissa?"

The brief moment of peace I'd been enjoying is replaced by a sudden, deep, sinking feeling.

"What the hell are you doing?"

10

We've all seen the situation a hundred times, in soaps, sitcoms, various films and television programmes, in dramas and comedies, pretty much any form of media. That perfectly curated scene, where two teenagers are caught by a parent at the most inopportune moment. Normally they're stark naked under a super-thin sheet, with perfect hair and makeup even though no one ever actually looks like that in those situations.

And while my trousers are in place, and I'm definitely not a teenager anymore, for a split second I feel a surge of embarrassment, a flush of shame at Freya having caught me literally red-handed, as two crimson tendrils of blood weave their way down towards my wrist. I'm instantly struck with the urge to hide the evidence of my indiscretion. But no sooner have I thought this, than those feelings are gone. After all, if there's anyone in this family who's got anything to feel guilty about, it sure as hell isn't me. And what am doing wrong, anyway? Trying to help a friend. Someone who's been there for me far more than she ever has.

"Is there something you want?" I demand. "I guess things like knocking on doors and respecting other people's privacy are beyond an alpha. I suppose that would demonstrate a level of decency that people who abandon their children don't normally have."

"Narissa," Calin hisses beside me. "There is no need for that."

"No, Calin, my daughter is right. I should have knocked. I didn't realise I'd be interrupting anything."

"You weren't," I say bluntly. "Calin's a vampire. He needs to feed."

"Yes. I understand."

That hard, alpha shell is starting to show cracks. I'm not going to lie; it's strangely satisfying to see.

"Is there something you want?" I ask again.

Her jaw is clenched, and I can see all the questions whirring behind her eyes, but in a blink, Freya draws her gaze away from me and the marks on my arm and turns to Calin.

"I wonder if you and I might have a word?" she says.

I don't know why her presence is grating on me so much. It wasn't this bad when we were in the village, talking about Alena, yet somehow just the sight of her here is enough to make my blood boil.

"Calin already told you there are no secrets between us. He's going to tell me everything you say to him, anyway. So, you might as well spit it out."

Calin turns to me.

CHAPTER 10

"It's okay," he says. "You stay here. Why don't you put some more wood on the fire? We're getting through it fast. Don't worry, we won't be long, will we?" He looks towards Freya.

"No, not long," my mother replies.

A moment later, the pair are gone and I'm on my own. Put some wood on the fucking fire. Really? Now I'm not just pissed at her. After all, there was no reason Calin couldn't have stood up for me. So much for not hiding anything from me.

It's tempting to follow them and try to listen in. After all, werewolves aren't meant to even like vampires. Whatever Freya wants with him, I know it can't be good. Nothing about her is good. And I don't like the power she wields over everyone either.

I'm still deciding whether I should go after them, when the door swings open.

"That didn't take long," I say. "What did she want?"

"So, the thing is—"

"Can you make this fast, Calin? I'd rather we get going now."

Freya stands in the doorway. Hovering. Waiting. That's when her words click into place.

"You're going somewhere?" I ask Calin.

He glances over his shoulder before taking a tentative step towards me.

"Yes. Your mo—Freya wants me to go to the town with her. See if I can pick up the scent of any of the other pack members. Or, possibly, any other vampires."

"Why now, and why do you need to go? She's a wolf. She can do that herself."

She steps into the cabin past Calin.

"Our sense of smell is only heightened when we're in wolf form, which is not how I can wander around town. If Calin is right about the vampires' involvement in our missing people, he's our best hope of getting a lead. Now, if you don't mind, we must get moving. We need as many night hours as possible."

As it happens, I do mind. Quite a lot.

"Sorry," I say, moving around to block her exit. "I know I've never been high on your list of priorities, only being your daughter and all, but what about me? Are you expecting me to just sit here, in the middle of a wood, on my own? Calin is here with *me*, remember? To protect *me*. Besides, why should he even trust you? Werewolves hate vampires."

"I trust her, Narissa," Calin says softly, his eyes meeting mine briefly before Freya interrupts again.

"There's nothing here you need protecting from," she says.

"I think I'll be the judge of that." I don't care if I do sound like a bitch.

Her lips twist and tighten, and her fingertips drum against her thighs. I can tell she wants to get out of here pronto, but there is no way I'm letting her sweep in and take control of everything.

"You don't feel safe here? Is that what you're saying, Narissa?"

I don't respond. I'm finding it hard to talk to the

woman right now. Unfortunately, she doesn't seem to be having that problem.

"When you returned to the village earlier this evening, how did you find your way? Louise and Calin arrived before you, so how did you manage it?"

"What are you on about?"

"You know exactly what. You followed his scent, didn't you? As a wolf."

Her gaze is scrutinising me, but it's a look I've inherited, and I throw it right back at her.

"What does it matter how I did it?" I reply.

"Can you just answer the question, Narissa. Did you come into the village as a wolf?"

"No. I was told that wasn't allowed."

"So, you changed back?"

"What are the twenty questions for?"

"Did you change at the boundary?"

"I'm sorry," I say. "I thought you were in a rush."

"Answer the question, Narissa."

I shake my head, exasperated. Maybe the fact that I've been spared years of this woman's torment is a good thing.

"Yes, I left here as a wolf, followed his scent and changed at the boundary. Why the hell does it matter? And why are you still here?"

"You changed at will that easily and you didn't flip back again at any point?"

"No. Of course I didn't."

She purses her lips.

"You can stay in the village tonight, while Calin's gone. Assuming that meets with your approval."

"What?"

"There's a small cabin you can use. It's been empty for quite a while, but you'll have Chrissie and her family next door. Not that I expect you to trust her either. Of course, if you should change in the village, there will be serious consequences."

I don't get it. I'm struggling to follow a single thread of logic from this woman.

"So now I'm allowed there? I thought the rules—"

"I am the Alpha. I *am* the rules. Now, do you want to stay here on your own, or do you want to overnight amongst the others?"

She doesn't even bother waiting for a response, just turns and strides out the door and into the forest.

"Great," I mutter to myself. What a fantastic hole I've dug myself into. Although, to be fair, a place with proper heating would probably improve my mood quite dramatically.

"Don't worry," Calin whispers in my ear. "You're safe. I would know if she were lying about anything."

"You didn't know when I was lying to you," I remind him.

With keeping warm still at the forefront of my mind, I make the decision to follow her, but that's not the only reason. There are cars in the village. I saw at least half a dozen. If I need to make a quick escape, stealing one of those might be my best option.

Leaving everything where it is, I head outside. Even in the dark, I notice a glimmer in her eyes.

"Our first run together," she says. "Are you ready?"

Oh hell no. I don't know how any of this pack bullshit works and I have zero intention of finding out. That includes going on group runs.

"You go ahead," I say. "Calin and I will follow. We have a few things to discuss first."

Disappointment flickers, but she doesn't ask again. She turns towards the forest and, in an instant, Freya disappears, and in her place is a wolf with pure white fur and rippling muscles, her eyes gleaming yellow. This is the Alpha. All powerful. A moment later, she's gone, and it's just me and Calin again.

"I'm sorry," he says. "I don't want to leave you, but it makes sense. Freya's right. The fact that Alena got away means that whoever took her could be looking for her. This might be the chance to get them. And there's the other factor too."

"What other factor?"

He pauses.

"The Vampire Council. They think I'm up here looking for the rogue vampire. That's my alibi for not being in London when—"

"I was broken out of the dungeon?"

In all my selfishness, I hadn't stopped to consider what his needs are in all this. He killed his own kind to save me, and if the Council finds out, it won't just be me they'll be hunting.

"Okay," I say, my voice cracking. "I get it. How long will you be gone?"

"Just a night or two. I have a room booked for me in town, anyway. I should spend at least a day there. Order some blood from Blackwatch. Make it all look legit."

My voice has gone altogether now. There's nothing I can say to object, yet the thought of him feeding from someone else makes this even harder.

"Okay," I say again.

He takes my hands gently in his.

"But if you need me to stay with you—"

"It's fine. I'll be fine. We should go."

He nods and glances towards the trees. When his eyes return to me, there's a different emotion in them. One I don't think I've ever seen before. Almost as if he's having fun.

"I don't suppose …"

"What?"

"Do you want to make it a race back?"

For a second, I think he's joking. Realising he's not, I'm about to refuse, when suddenly the thought of running with Calin seems so much more appealing than the offer to run with Freya. The wolf is niggling in the back of my head, not a growl though, more a bark. Like this could be an adventure.

"Okay, let's do it!"

11

We speed through the undergrowth, our feet barely touching the ground. My body is low, and my muscles are loving the burn. In front of me, Calin is pulling ahead. Just a few metres at first, but the gap is widening. Trying to keep up with him has my lungs heaving. As I jump the stream, I lose sight of him entirely. I realise that, while I've seen him appear and disappear at speed before, I've never actually witnessed a vampire running. Not that this should be surprising. It would be pretty hard to race around like this in public and remain inconspicuous. It's probably in the vampire book of no-nos. He's older than me, I remind myself, and while he's outpacing me now, maybe with a bit of practice, I'd be able to keep up with him.

I quash the thought. This is not going to be a regular thing. Wolf is not who I am. I am human. This is a one-off, well maybe a second one-off, that's all. Besides, if I stay in the village, there'll be no need for me to ever turn into this thing again. No need to come into the forest at all. That thought is bouncing around my head as I reach the boundary.

With my sharper vision, I can focus clearly on things much further away. Ahead are the silhouettes of two people. I don't need to be able to see Freya's expression to know she's watching me. Waiting to see how difficult it is for me to transform back. Of course, this could all be part of some ploy to catch me out. I get the distinct feeling she'd love it if I failed, but there's no way I'm going to give her the satisfaction.

I immediately start to think of the most human things I can.

A cold beer in a pub garden on a hot summer's day, condensation running down the glass as I take a long draw. Brushing my teeth with mint toothpaste. Peppermint, though. I've never understood people who like spearmint.

I have just begun to imagine a Mr Whippy ice cream with hundreds and thousands on the top and a flake sticking out of the side, when a voice interrupts me.

"Impressive," she says, "Although I would expect no less, given your heritage. Now, let's take you to your place."

By place, Freya means a cabin on the edge of the settlement. It's old, wooden and, from the look of it, hasn't been inhabited for years. Compared to her home and most of the buildings around, it's a big step down, and I'm surprised they haven't demolished it. The windows are small and the paint on the frames is peeling. The door is average looking but is held in place with large hinges, at least three times normal size but covered in rust. Even if my so-called heritage doesn't stretch to a place like hers, it's a step up from the hut in the woods,

"This has heating?" I check.

"There are geothermal vents all around this area. It's why our ancestors settled here in the first place. Be careful in the shower. The water gets pretty hot."

I don't know if she's joking or not.

"The lock sticks. Just jiggle the key a bit," she says, lifting up a planter to retrieve a poorly concealed key and demonstrating what she means until the door clicks open. "And make sure that it's secured properly before you go anywhere."

"I didn't think you'd bother with things like locking doors," I respond. "Not with the whole community-family-pack thing you've got going here."

"Everyone needs their privacy, Narissa."

The door's now open, but she's still standing in front of it.

"Like I said before, Chrissie is next door if you need anything. Or if you want to go for a run—"

"I won't."

"Well, if you change your mind—"

"I won't," I repeat, cutting in. Thankfully, she's not stupid enough to push it. Considering that only a few minutes ago she was in a massive rush to get Calin out of here, I'm confused by all this loitering.

"Treat this like it's your home," she says. "The room, the village. It's all open to you. And, as for the things … well, it's up to you what you do with them."

"Things?"

She moves back, finally allowing me a glimpse into the cabin beyond.

Even in the gloom, it's easy to tell nobody has stepped foot in here for years. There's a thick veneer of dust coating the floor, and cobwebs everywhere. The dust bunnies are almost as big as real-life ones. There's a bed in the corner—an actual bed, as opposed to a mattress on the floor—and a small kitchenette. Then I notice half-a-dozen brown, cardboard boxes stacked beneath the window. There's nothing special about them; they look like any normal packing boxes you would use to move house or store a few surplus bits and pieces in. And yet I'm drawn to them. I walk slowly over, reach out and flip open the lid of the first one.

A gasp catches in my throat as I see what's inside. Dozens of small, leather notebooks.

"You took them," I say. "You took them all."

12

Freya and Calin have gone. Had I any sense, I would have chased after them, yelling and demanding explanations. I should have turned into a wolf and pinned her to the ground and refused to let her go until she told me the truth. But the sight of those leather-bound notebooks rendered me numb. Even now, after almost an hour staring at them, I can't bring myself to read them.

This cabin is certainly warmer than the one in the woods, and there's a small sofa onto which I've tipped the first box of diaries. That's as far as I've got.

The aroma of dust and leather mingles as I pick one up and run my fingers over the creases on the cover. How many years have I longed to see these again? How many times did I plead with Jessop, the Head of Blackwatch, to return them, beg him for just one memento of my father? *It doesn't matter if you don't believe me about the vampire. But please, please, let me have the diaries. Even just one. I would never show it to anyone.* What difference would it have made to them? My father had already told me all about vampires and the Council and blood donors. All I wanted was the chance to hold those little brown books full of his notes and drawings and remember him sitting in his armchair, scribbling away. God, how I'd despised Jessop for keeping them from me. He'd told me at least a dozen times that they didn't have them, but I never believed him. Who else would have taken them? And now I know. It was Freya. It had always been her.

AT SOME POINT LAST NIGHT, I fell asleep. I don't know when. I never even made it over to the bed. Waking up, my neck is aching from the awkward angle it's been resting at on the arm of the sofa. Light is streaming through the windows, past the curtains I forgot to close. One of the notebooks is lying open next to me. Stretching out the cricks in my neck and shoulders, I pull up my legs and rest the book against my knees.

November '08
    Shortage of donors. The ones we are using are so ... desperate. I worry their bodies are too frail to deal with the stress. But what other choice do we have?

. . .

CHAPTER 12

I FLICK BACK a couple of pages.

MORE INTERVIEWS THIS WEEK. Jessop wants me to help. Sit in on the panel. Monitor reactions. I'll need to think of something. The ones recently have been so aggressive. So desperate for promotion they don't even care what the job is. He thinks I don't know that even at their starting wage they'll be on more than I earn now. It's not worth an argument though. I take my salary in silence.

IT'S A STRANGE LINE, but I'm not awake enough to try and analyse it yet.

After skimming through a few more pages, I land upon a picture. A flower. It's just sketched in biro, but there's such fluidity in the strokes that I can almost see the breeze rippling the petals. When I was little, I thought he was the most magnificent artist. That he should sell his paintings and they'd fetch millions of pounds, and we'd never have to worry about money again.

My thoughts wander to the rest of the boxes. Are they all full of diaries? Possibly, although I can't remember there being that many of them. Still stiff, I move to open another one, when there's a rap on the door.

"Narissa, are you in there? It's Lou. I went to the cabin, to see if you were okay, but you weren't there, so I came back and Mum said that you were down here because the vampire had gone with Freya and that you were allowed to stay in the village, even though you've only just turned, which is seriously, freaking cool!"

There's no way I'm ready to deal with her face-to-face, but after a moment's consideration, I decide it's better than talking to her through wood. I get the feeling that if I don't respond soon, she'd hammer her way through it. I open the door.

"Lou."

The sun's blinding. I squint and lift my hand, trying to shade my eyes a little.

"Great, you're up. Here, I brought you coffee. There's probably instant in there somewhere, but it'll be well old. We have a pretty decent machine in our place. Mum bought it in town. It's easily the best in the village. She has a problem now, though. Needs at least four a day. She'd kill me for saying that, but honestly if she doesn't—"

"Thanks, I'll take the coffee," I say and reach out for the mug. When I go to push the door shut again, her foot catches it.

She looks awkward and, for a second, I think she blocked it by mistake, until I notice she's nervously chewing her bottom lip

"What do you want, Lou?" I ask.

"I don't mean to interrupt whatever you're doing. I know it's all a bit crazy around here, but would we be able to come in? Just for a minute? There's something we need to ask you. I know it's probably not a convenient time, but it won't take long."

At the use of the word, "we", I notice someone is

standing behind her: male, about my age, possibly a couple of years younger but definitely older than her. His hair is reddish-brown, his eyes a greeny-blue. The resemblance between the pair is striking.

"This is my brother, Arthur," she says.

I study him for a moment longer before turning my attention back to her. "What's this about?" I say. "What do you want?"

"We just need to ask you one thing, then we'll be gone. Oh, actually, we have something to tell you, too."

I want to say no. I want them to leave me alone to get on with reading my dad's diaries, but strangely enough, I already like the girl, and the fact that she's managing not to speak while I contemplate her request suggests this thing might be worth hearing. It's certainly the longest I've known her to be silent.

Taking a sip from the coffee, I move back for them to enter. Arthur closes the door behind him.

"Wow," Lou says, moving towards the sofa and the notebooks. "What are these? There are loads of them. I love the leather. Are they diaries? Are they yours? I didn't think you brought anything with you. Or are they Freya's?"

"What they are is none of your business," I say.

A flash of hurt crosses her face but doesn't stick. They're the ones intruding on me. They should expect a little curtness, particularly at this time of the morning.

"What is it you want?" I try again. "You've got two minutes. I've got some important things to do." Not technically true, but hey.

"There is no easy way of saying this," Lou starts, looking nervous again. "And I don't want you to think that we are being rude. Or that it matters to me, personally. Or to Arthur—it doesn't matter to either of us, honestly. We are fine. We have no issue with it. It would just help to know, that's all. But it really doesn't matter."

"What doesn't matter?"

"It's just, if it's true, then … you know. But maybe you don't even know yourself. But we should really know, so—"

"Are you Freya's daughter?" Arthur interrupts his sister. "Is the Alpha your mother?"

He stares at me, waiting for an answer, something flickering in his expression. Cold or just wary, perhaps. I guess my heritage really might be important if a werewolf a full foot taller than me is looking agitated about it.

"Why does it matter?" I'm deliberately nonchalant as I flop down onto the sofa. "What difference does it make who my family is?"

The pair exchange a look, making no attempt to hide their fear. When Lou turns back to me, she's gone pale.

"It matters quite a lot. Because if you are Freya's daughter, then they're going to want you dead."

13

For a full second, there's absolute silence. The drained look in Lou's face deepens and the fear in Arthur's eyes is shining bright and clear. Someone wants to kill me or, to be more precise, someone else wants to kill me. The thought feels like the punchline to another joke. Whether it's a sign of stress or anxiety, I find myself laughing.

"What? What's funny?" Lou asks.

"This isn't a joke. We're not messing around," Arthur adds.

"Of course you're not. But, you see, I've come here to get away from non-humans who want to kill me. And now it turns out I've arrived somewhere where more non-humans want to kill me."

"Firstly," Arthur glowers, "we are human. We've got all the human bits. Just some extras as well. Secondly, you still haven't answered our question. Are you Freya's daughter?"

"Daughter is a loose term," I reply.

"What does that mean?"

As much as I like Lou, I've decided I dislike Arthur an equal amount. Gut instinct or otherwise, something about him just doesn't sit right with me. Still, it's apparent they're not going anywhere until they've got this off their chests, and it would probably be a good idea to find out who else wants me dead.

"Loose, means that my relationship with Freya starts and ends with biology. She hasn't been an actual mother to me for the last twenty years and she's sure as hell not going to start being one now. So, if anyone has a problem with that, they can take it up with her. Or not. I honestly don't care. I don't want to be here, and I certainly don't want to be a wolf. Believe me, as soon as I can get things sorted, I will be out of your hair—or fur."

While I think I've explained myself rather eloquently, considering how pissed off I am, the two of them are still standing there.

"You need to understand—" Lou starts.

"No. *You* need to understand," I interrupt. "I don't even know who you are. And, believe me, you know absolutely nothing about me. About who I am or what I've been through. So, when you come in here, in my face, making assumptions ..." I pause. It's not that I don't have more to say, but my wolf is growling so loudly, it's drowning out the rest of the thoughts in my head. Sucking in a long, deep breath, I close my eyes and force it down. When I open them again, Arthur is staring at me.

He straightens his back before extending his hand. "Look, I can see we got off on the wrong foot. Let's try again. I'm Art, Lou's brother."

He pauses partly to take a breath but mostly to see if I'll take his hand. When I don't, he casually withdraws it and continues.

"We would like to know about you. If you'd like to tell us. Would I be right in thinking that you didn't grow up knowing you were a wolf?"

He enunciates each word, like he's worried I'll have difficulty understanding. Still, I decide to play along. For a little bit, at least.

"I grew up not even knowing that they existed. Vampires, yes. Wolves, no."

"Interesting. How come?"

"Not that it's any of your business, but my father was Blackwatch."

"Was?"

"Was."

He doesn't take that any further but runs his fingers through his hair before continuing.

"Well, werewolf is in your blood, obviously. For us, it's more than that. We're born to it. It's in our blood but also all around us in the air we breathe, the food we eat and—"

"The grass you piss on, I get it. But I've already said I'm not a threat to anyone out there. I don't even want to be part of this."

"Don't you see, that doesn't help. Life here, this pack, people would give their lives to defend it."

"And I'm not a risk to any of that."

"Why would they believe you? You said yourself, you don't want to be part of it. You've no loyalty. You're an outsider."

"So, you're saying that to be safe, I need to let them know I'm Freya's daughter?"

"No!"

"No!"

They shout simultaneously, rendering me well and truly confused. Scratching my head, I try again to figure it out.

"I thought you said they'd kill me to protect this place?"

"No, I didn't. I said they'd give their lives for it. They are not the ones you have to worry about."

Lou coughs in an unsubtle way and it sounds like she says a name under her breath, something like David. Or Daniel perhaps. Lifting my hand to my head, I look to Art for some clarification.

"Well, what do I need to do? How do I convince this … whoever, that I'm not a risk?"

"You won't," he says. "To him you're a risk just being here. You threaten what he's trying to build his future on."

"But it's just him?

"Daniel is the main one," Lou says. "But he has groupies, gammas that fall in and out of favour. They're not at all well liked."

"Previously, the Alpha would have removed them before they became too big a problem," Arthur adds.

"Removed them?" I realise what he means before I've even finished asking. "That's not done now, then?"

Lou shakes her head. "Freya put an end to all that."

"Which is good in some ways but in others, well ... a bit of tough love can be useful now and then. I guess she never imagined this situation would occur."

Rubbing his head, Art appears to mull something over before speaking again.

"Right now, no one can touch you. Before you arrived, Freya said that a new wolf would be coming, and that she was to be supported. As long as your mum's the Alpha, her rules stand and you're safe. But if they sense she has a weakness ..."

The reason for their concern suddenly registers.

"You're not here because you're worried for me. You're worried for Freya. About someone using me against her."

"We're worried about everything," Lou says. "The missing pack members, Alena turning up injured and then dying. Our mother."

"Your mother?"

"New alphas tend to want a whole new leadership team."

The way Art and Lou speak, I can tell they've been finishing each other's sentences for years.

"And let's just say, if Daniel comes into power, he's unlikely to let our mother step down gracefully. He and his followers are now telling people that Freya shouldn't be Alpha anymore. Last night they started commenting on how she ought to be here with us and should have sent others into town with the vampire. People are scared, and frightened people are easy to manipulate. If they know that she has a weakness—"

"You mean me."

"It might be enough for him to incite a coup."

"Wow," I say, probably not the most appropriate word, but it's all that I can manage. This week just keeps getting better and better.

"I know this sounds scary," Art says, moving next to me. "But you have to realise that this is the nature of a pack. This is what happens. Trust me, your mum has fought off contenders a dozen times, if not more. As long as she's the right person to lead, she'll keep winning."

"But we don't want it to come to that. Not with everything else that's going on," Lou says. "Not until we know what's happening."

"Okay." I rub the bridge of my nose. "What do I do? Not tell people, Freya is my ...?" I still can't manage to say it, even if they can. "I shouldn't let people know we're related. Is that what you're saying?"

"Definitely," Lou says. "Don't tell anyone."

"And if anyone asks. Say you were found on Dartmoor. Say you were left as a baby."

"Dartmoor? Why there?"

"That's the only other place in the UK where there's a pack. If they think you were found there, then everyone will assume you were dumped by one of their pack. It will throw them off the scent."

"Talking of which," Lou says. "Remember, when you are in wolf form, your thoughts are open to others if you can't block them. You could give something away. If you want to go for a run, you could go with one of us, or Mum. We don't mind, do we, Art? We can choose a quiet time."

She mentioned something about blocking before but I don't want to get into that now.

"Any more rules you want to give me?" I ask, my voice laden with sarcasm, which she doesn't seem to pick up on.

"Do you want to grab one of those notebooks?" she asks.

14

Despite Lou's inability to read my tone, Art thankfully catches on fast.

"Lou, how about we give Narissa some space for now," he says, gesturing towards the door. "We'll have plenty of time later to fill her in on everything."

"Oh, yes, sorry." Lou's cheeks colour just a fraction. "I tend to get carried away."

"It's fine," I say. "Maybe in a couple of days?"

"Yeah? Great. Whenever is good for you. Just let me know. Or Art. Or Mum."

"I will do."

She's about to say something else, when Art practically pushes her out of the door. I assume he's going to follow straight after her, but he pauses.

"I realise you don't know me," he says, digging his hands into his pockets. "You don't know anyone here yet, but most of us are good people. At least we try to be. If you need anything, you can always come to me, or my mum. Or your mum, too." He shakes his head. "Honestly, I don't get her leaving you. Aunty Freya helped raise me. She's one of the most compassionate people I've ever met."

"Let's be honest, living in this place, you probably haven't met that many people, have you?"

He chuckles at my comment which was, I suppose, the desired effect. However, I realise it's not much of a joke. I can't imagine living here allows for a great social life.

"You're right," he says. "We're relatively sheltered here. But I grew up without a dad. Lots of us here have. And I know it's not easy. You expect things from parents, and when they don't deliver … it's tough. So, I do get it. And, like we said, if you need to talk …"

It's hard to respond to a comment like that. I never expected anything from my mother. How could I? I thought she was dead.

"Anyway, the offer's there. It would be good to go for a run together sometime, if you fancy it."

"Thank you," I say, thinking that I maybe judged him just a little too quickly. "But I'm giving the whole wolf thing a miss."

My words cause a growl to rumble through my head, but I shut it down. The wolf doesn't get a say in what I do. Not now, not ever.

Removing his hands from his pockets, Arthur combs his fingers through his hair and for the first time since entering the cabin, smiles. It's genuine and infectious and I wonder how many she-wolves have fallen for it.

"I'll be interested to see how long that lasts. I get the feeling you could be an awesome wolf," he says, then leaves, closing the door behind him.

I stand there, thinking about his last comment. Would I be an awesome wolf? The chances are slim. I was a distinctly average human. Maybe that's unfair. I was above average at things like manipulating my friends and getting myself into deep shit that I had no way of getting out of. Below average at most other things.

The quiet is deafening after Art and Lou's departure, leaving far too much scope for rumination. Someone wants to overthrow Freya? If what they said is true, and it's all part and parcel of this life, then that's another reason why I want nothing to do with this place. She's not my concern. I am. But, if something happens to her, then what about me? I can't believe they'd kill me, when I'm obviously no threat at all. But, then again, forty-eight hours ago, I wouldn't have believed I was a wolf …

What I need is a distraction, and thankfully, I've got half-a-dozen boxes full of them. Perhaps my parents met by accident, like Calin and Chrissie. Or maybe it was through Blackwatch. It could have been in a formal, arranged meeting. However, Oliver never mentioned werewolves, so that seems unlikely. But who knows? Hopefully, it's written down somewhere in one of these diaries.

With the first box I opened full of Dad's last entries, I go straight for the bottom one, hoping I'll find some of the older books. The tape has been stuck there for so long that it takes half the cardboard lid with it when I peel it off. Closing my eyes, I let the aroma wash over me once more. I could never have imagined how much this smell of leather would remind me of my dad. Now it's something I'll never forget.

Taking out another of the diaries, I open it up and start to read.

Nov 4 '95

I don't know if I can believe what I think I just saw. Maybe I'm on some kind of hallucinogenic. Maybe they drugged us. It would have been entirely possible to put something in the jugs of water. I have no recollection of how much I drank. But that was hours ago. Surely the effects should be wearing off by now. I'm home in the flat, but my mind will be stuck in that building for a long, long time. Those teeth ... those claws ... It must be some form of interview technique. The ones who were already part of Blackwatch acted like it was all so normal but it was like something out of a science fiction story. There was another interviewee there from the police force. Jessop I think he said his name was. He looked like I felt. Confused. Scared. We've arranged to meet up for a drink. Maybe we can work out what their plan is with all this. What they hope to achieve.

Nov 5 '95

Jessop is sure it's a training device. He's heard of them utilising similar techniques in Europe so he's not concerned. As he pointed out there's no way those things could exist without the rest of the world knowing. I guess they've all been having a laugh at our expense. Not sure this is the type of organisation I want to work for if that's how they get their kicks but I'll see the interview process through.

Nov 8 '95
It's real! It's all real!

I SCAN through the next few pages, which basically comprise more of the same. More disbelief. More fear. More talk of if he really wants to be accepted into Blackwatch, not to mention what might happen if he doesn't now he's got this far, been told so much. As I know the outcome, I scan through to the end of the book, where he's joined the training programme. No further reference to werewolves comes up. Dropping the book, I pick up the next one.

APRIL '96
Have been given role of collating donor information. Bluntly put it's a desk job. An exceptionally dull desk job. Any fears I had about working here and being viscously attacked by a vampire have been completely nullified after spending all day chained to a desk. We see them during training of course but mostly it's less action than in the police force for the same pay but with more secrecy. I'm not sure I could go back to the force now though. Not with the things I know. Others do get to go on missions. Hush-hush missions. I guess it's a case of biding my time here until they think I'm suitable to move up beyond the job of desk clerk.

CHAPTER 14

. . .

AGAIN, I skim pages. There's more about the training. About the day-to-day jobs. About Jessop and the others he works with, too. They're all things I'd be interested in reading about if I wasn't looking for something specific. With my legs becoming simultaneously numb and itchy, I move from the sofa to the bed, taking the diary with me. This cabin may be substantially bigger than the one in the woods, but it feels like it's getting smaller by the minute.

As the day passes, I skim through more of my dad's entries, but it's more of the same. Desk work. There's the occasional mention of vampires. If werewolf powers gave me a super-fast reading ability, I wouldn't have to waste so much time on donor protocols.

I'm almost at the end of another book and ready to toss it aside, when the word I've been looking for leaps off the page at me. Shuffling back on the bed, my heart is thudding as I start to read.

JULY '96

Probation is over. In three weeks Jessop and I are being sent on our first mission together. To say I'm nervous would be an understatement. Learning about vampires was one thing but now they've thrown werewolves into the mix too. Data on them is exceptionally limited but they don't sound the friendliest bunch. From what I can tell Blackwatch has had no communication with them for nearly a century. Let's hope we don't screw this up.

. . .

JULY '96

Just one week to go and it's been confirmed. Jessop and I are going to be the ones to make contact. He's excited by this but is refusing to recognise the glaringly obvious. We are the most expendable operatives in the organisation. Blackwatch is sending up lambs to the wolves. I guess in a sense I can understand it. No wives. No families. We live for work so why not choose us to put our lives on the line? I guess the thing is I'd never really thought about family until I accepted this job but over these recent days I can barely think about anything else. Unfortunately with this route my life has taken I just don't see how it will be possible. How could anyone keep a relationship together while spinning so many lies?

THE NOTEBOOK ENDS on the following page. I grab the next one from the pile, but it's marked *Feb '05* and he's talking about being posted to London with missions taking place near familiar landmarks. Knowing it's well past what I'm after, I drop it on the floor and pick up another. *April '05*. Digging a little deeper, I pull out one from Sept '04 and think that the earlier ones must be at the bottom of the box, But soon it's sitting there empty, and none have been even close to the date in ninety-six when he was about to visit the wolves.

It's okay, I say to myself. *I've got plenty of time.*

I'm a patient person. I was hunting Styx for years before I finally found him. And true, it was touch and go there for a while, but I got him in the end. There's no

CHAPTER 14

way I'm going to let a set of boxes get the better of me, but it feels like the room is getting even smaller, and my own agitation is being amplified by the wolf's.

I tear open another box and yet another. Before I know it, I'm on the final one, tossing unwanted diaries to one side as soon as I've checked the dates on the first page and still not finding another from 1996 or thereabouts. With each discarded notebook, my patience frays further.

When I reach the very last dairy, my fingers grip the leather with such force that my knuckles turn white. This has to be it. This could have the answers. But even before I open it, I know I'm going to be disappointed. The dates are from the late noughties.

Where are they? The question goes around and around in my head. Why are the notebooks containing those missing dates not here? My gut squirms and I realise I already know the answer. She's responsible. Without a shadow of a doubt, Freya is behind it, making sure I don't get any more information than she is prepared to let me to have.

"Screw you, Freya!" I yell.

Inside my head, the wolf growls with fury, causing my anger to burn even brighter. Both of us want justice. We deserve it. The leather twists in my hands. I stiffen. I was about to rip the spine off the notebook. My dad's diary. I wanted to destroy it for a moment. The thought is a sobering one. The memory of him sitting there, scribbling away, pushes down the wolf, but only by a fraction.

Using all the willpower I have, I throw the book to one side and pick up the nearest cushion which I rip in two without a second's thought. Feathers fly up in an explosion of white and the shredded fabric drops from my hands. That one ruined, I pick up another and then a third. Every spray of feathers helps.

"Screw you, Freya!" I call again into the fog of down that is drifting all around me. "Screw you and your pack."

When I finally stop and drop to my knees, I realise I'm panting. My hands are slick with sweat, and the cabin is full of small, white plumes. The carpet, the counter tops, everything is covered. It looks like a fox has gone mad in a chicken coop, although wolf would probably be a more accurate analogy. Still breathless, I'm pushing myself up onto my feet, when there's another knock at the door.

"I'm busy!" I yell.

The last thing I can deal with right now is Art and Lou pestering me with more conspiracy theories.

Whoever it is obviously can't read the tone of my voice. Two seconds later, another knock comes.

Flexing my hands, I go and open the door.

"What do you want?" I snap.

Looking only a fraction less weary than she did the night before, Chrissie is dressed in denim shorts and a white vest. Her long, grey hair is loose. Her eyes move past me.

"Decorating?" she enquires, with a twinkle in her eye.

I move to block the view.

"Sorry, I don't mean to interrupt, but your mother asked me to check on you."

"Well, you can tell you did that."

She presses her lips together.

"How are you doing?" she asks, her eyes returning to the room. "Don't worry, we all experience caged-wolf syndrome now and again."

"Caged wolf?"

"It's hard to stay indoors for extended periods of time. Some people say it's because of Eve, you know, because of how she was kept captive for so long. Whatever the reason, it's certainly not in our nature to stay confined. I don't mean to pry. I'm certain you're fine."

There's no question there, but she pauses as if she's waiting for me to reply. When I don't, she speaks again.

"I've not got anything on right now, if you'd like to go for a run. Or a walk?"

Caged-wolf syndrome; I can't help feeling the truth of it. The walls have been feeling like they've been closing in on me for some time now, and if I don't do something about it soon, it might not just be the pillows that end up shredded. But I can control this. Trying not to grind my teeth, I look back at the mess and then at Chrissy.

"I'm not changing to a wolf," I say bluntly.

"A human walk is just fine with me, although I've got a roast on. You don't mind if we check on it first, do you? Or we could just eat, if you're hungry?"

15

Hungry doesn't even come close to describing how I'm feeling, I realise as I step outside the cabin and lock the door. Just the mention of a roast and my stomach is growling and my mouth watering at the thought of something hot and cooked, and I don't even care what sort of roast it is. I don't remember when my last meal was. There's a good chance I haven't eaten properly since before I went to the Blood Bank with Rey. Right now, I'd eat roast rabbit with the fur still on, although that thought makes me a little nervous. The wolf better not be taking control of my tastebuds, too. That would really piss me off.

Outside, the breeze has a warmth to it.

"What time is it?" I ask.

"About five," Chrissie replies, then adds with a smile, "Why, did you have somewhere else to be?"

Ignoring the riposte, I follow her up the stairs into the next-door cabin.

CHAPTER 15

"Will Lou and Art be in?"

"Arthur?" She stops on the steps. "When did you meet him? Did he come bothering you?"

"Really, it was nothing."

Seeming to disagree, Chrissy shakes her head with a huff.

"I'm sorry. I don't know what to do with that one. He can't leave well enough alone. And Lou follows him around blindly. I hope they didn't say anything to upset you?"

I go to wave the question away but stop myself.

"So, is it true what they said ... about my—" I cut myself short. "About Freya?"

Chrissie's lips twist.

"How about we chat over some food?" she finally says.

The moment we enter the front door, the smell hits me. Meat, vegetables, a full carvery of aromas fills the room. One that is substantially bigger and better furnished than I would have expected.

"You've got so much equipment. How do you have enough electricity to run it all?" I ask, noting the industrial-sized fridge and large cooker.

"Solar panels, mostly. We've got good engineers amongst us and built up a substantial network over the years. Things like the fridge we pick up on our trips to town. We need plenty of capacity to store food over the winter, in case we get cut off. We take good care of things, and they tend to last us a fair while.

"Now, root around and find us some plates and

cutlery. They're all in the cupboard over there. I'll get this bird out and dish up."

Following her instructions, I find everything we need and set out the dining- table.

"Are you sure we shouldn't wait for the others?" I ask. "Won't Art and Lou expect to join you?"

Holding the largest baking tin I've ever seen, Chrissy raises an eyebrow. "Are you serious? If those two had known there was a goose in the oven, we'd have come back to a pile of bones, and plates piled up in the sink. They're plenty big enough to sort themselves out. Now tell me, leg or breast?"

As far as I'm aware, it's my first time eating goose. And it's good. Fat drips down my chin and I have to force myself to slow down. Rather than the hunger abating, this delicious food only seems to be making it worse. Picking up a leg, I tear at the meat with my teeth, before remembering my manners and putting it down again. Pausing, I make myself finish my glass of water before taking up my knife and fork and returning to the meat. My hands are trembling. I just can't get the food into me quickly enough.

"Don't feel you have to be polite in this house," Chrissy assures me, topping up my plate. "Trust me, my kids aren't."

Resisting the urge to resort to my hands again, I persist with the cutlery. Little by little, my appetite is satiated.

"Is it true?" I ask, when I can finally concentrate on something other than eating. "There's a wolf who doesn't want Freya in charge? Who wants to take over? And some people support him?"

"So that's what Art and Lou went to you about."

"But are they right? Is she in danger with me here?"

The noise Chrissie makes is somewhere between a snort and laugh. It's definitely meant to be derisive.

"Can I ask you something, Narissa?" she says, leaning towards me.

"I suppose so," I reply, although I don't feel like this is going to be good.

"How many people that you know in London are content with their lives there?"

I put my cutlery down.

"Sorry? I don't follow you."

"How many people are perfectly happy? Did you know anyone who was? Just humour me here. It'll make sense."

Abandoning my food, I consider the question. Thinking of how I earlier ridiculed Arthur for his diminutive social circle, I don't think I was really in any place to comment. Mine isn't much better. In fact, it's probably worse. I'm still thinking about my answer when Chrissie continues.

"People here are generally happy. Very happy. But we are a community and a sizeable one at that. And in any community, it's impossible to please everyone. That's a sad fact. But another one is that your mother does an exceptional job, even more so considering it's one she never wanted in the first place and that came with a burden most of us could never even contemplate. The burden of leaving you behind."

"But she didn't have to. She could have brought me with her. Me *and* Dad. He would have come with her in a heartbeat. I know he would. The way he always spoke about her …"

A lump comes to my throat as I recall how he would flick through old albums. Almost all the photos were taken with an instant camera. Some of the prints had become so faded that they were sepia in tone and so often handled, their edges were almost translucent. He didn't have many, and at least those weren't taken when he died. But they're back in my flat in London, and I doubt I'll ever get to see them again.

"Your mother was given an impossible choice. Believe me. I was the one who tried to comfort her in her grief. As daughter to an alpha, she saw things, was made to do things as a young wolf that she just couldn't live with. Which is why she ran away. She was terrified that it would be just the same for you, if she brought you into this life."

"So, better to just leave me to the foster care system if anything should happen to my one, remaining parent?"

"In her mind, yes. Honestly, I can't explain her rationale, other than to promise you that there was one. And I can assure you that every day, every hour away from you, was torture for her."

So much so she couldn't even pick up a phone? I want to say. And it must have been torture having this whole crew of people running around at her beck and call.

"Look, let's not talk about this now," Chrissie says, sitting back in her chair, obviously attempting to try and lighten the mood. "This shouldn't be coming from me, anyway. Why don't we head out for that walk? And no pressure of course, the offer of a run is still there."

Although I want to refuse, the prickling beneath my skin has grown more intense this past hour spent with Chrissie. But rather than an angry clawing, it seems more like excitement. Like when I was about to race with Calin. It's as if my inner wolf is enjoying being around another, even one in human form. Besides, would it be that bad? Just a quick run, like the couple I did yesterday. Those short bursts calmed the wolf enough that I got through the night okay. Maybe even just five minutes at most ...

16

I want to hate this, I really do. But I can't.

It's like water when you're parched.

No, it's more vital than that. It's like oxygen. Oxygen for the wolf.

Last night, when I just needed to get somewhere fast, I hadn't realised this. Not fully. I didn't appreciate the softness of the grass or the spring in the earth beneath my feet. Or the thousand distinct aromas that come to me with every breath. Or the subtle whisper of the air as it passes gently through my fur. It's as if nature is singing to me with every stride that I take.

Okay, I sound like I prat. I get that. Even in my own head, it seems idiotic. But this is ... freedom. That's the only way to describe it.

As we approached the well, Chrissie transformed first while I hovered for a moment, somehow knowing it was the right thing to do. Then half a dozen people waltzed naked out of the undergrowth, like they'd been told they needed to leave immediately. A few glared at me, but others threw brief, fleeting smiles. I ignored the former, tried to reciprocate the latter and then, taking a deep breath, stepped into the wood and transformed.

What was strange this time was how fleeting the pain was. Sure, I felt every one of my bones snap and reform, every tendon and muscle shred and regrow, but there was a weird satisfaction to it. Like my body now knew what it was doing and accepted it, was almost looking forward to it.

I immediately picked up on Chrissie's scent and ran towards it. Her amber fur was vibrant, glistening as it reflected the colours of the autumn leaves around us. With a dip of her muzzle, I knew what she was telling me to do. To follow her. To run.

So that's what I've been doing for the last two hours. Just running. I've sped past trees and plants that I've never noticed before, but I can pick each out individually just from its scent. I've leapt over brooks and even—now don't judge me for this—chased a rabbit. Yes, I know, huge cliché, but what can I say? It was fun. And this forest ... it's immense.

Every few minutes, I force myself to stop and take stock of where I am and what I can see, to maintain my bearings. The village has its own distinct smell—in that there's a heavy concentration of people there—and I'm pretty sure I could find my way back at a push if I had to. Not that I need worry. Chrissie is beside me the entire time. Sometimes, I can almost *feel* her presence. As if the wolf parts of us are calling to one another, but every time I try to focus on this feeling, it evaporates.

It's late evening when she finally comes to rest in a small clearing. Almost instantly, she morphs from wolf to woman. Assuming this is so we can talk, I do the same.

This is my first time standing out in the open with a stranger, naked, and it's seriously weird, I can tell you. There again, there are all sorts of spas and retreats where this would be regarded as perfectly normal, right? So, really, it's the same, only free. Just an exclusive resort but with no spa facilities and where people change between wolf and human. Brilliant.

"So how was that?" Chrissie asks, a mixture of worry and anticipation in her face. "I take it you enjoyed yourself?"

"I just can't believe how easy it is," I reply, honestly. "Or how fast I am. This is probably the most exercise I've done in my entire life."

She grins. "I'm glad you like it." Then a look of concern hovers for a moment before she blinks it away. "We should head back now. Your mother was planning to return from town just after sunset."

My insides do a small somersault.

"What about Calin? Is he coming back too?"

"I assume so, although I'm not sure."

I nod, trying not to give away how much I want to see him, but I suspect it's obvious.

"Come on," she says. "We'll go back a different way. The more you explore, the quicker you'll remember the layout of the place, and the more at home you'll feel."

Home? This is not my home and won't ever be, part of me wants to say to set the record straight, just in case she's thinking otherwise. But I don't want to ruin the mood, and so I stay silent and transform back to the wolf.

We head back more slowly. The evening has brought out a whole host of new animals, with scents that my nose just can't help but take an interest in. We weave our way over new terrain—rocks and scrubland as well as the grassy forest. As the sun sets, we are still running, noses to the ground. With each step, the aroma of the village is growing stronger, and as the moon rises above the trees, we reach the edge of the forest, and it comes into view below us. Changing back to human form, I grab one of the garments from the well. This time I luck out with a dress.

"Do these belong to anyone in particular?" I ask, slipping it over my head.

"Not really, and there are so many comings and goings it's rare you'll end up with nothing A couple of people have the responsibility of making sure there are always enough things available."

"And no one minds you helping yourself?"

"People aren't precious about things like that here. Clothes are just clothes."

That's a nice attitude. I like it. I should run some of things up here that Lou brought me. There are far more in the bags than I need.

Back at the house, Lou and Art are already tucking into the remainder of the roast.

"You went for a run, didn't you?"

The verbal barrage starts the moment I step through the door.

"I knew you would," Lou says, "I know you thought you didn't want to, but it's amazing, isn't it? And did Mum drive you insane? I bet she was all up in your head, wasn't she? It's infuriating when she does that—asking you loads of questions or trying to correct your running technique."

However irritating she may be, I can't help but smile at her.

"We spent most of time running, so we couldn't really talk that much."

"You mean other than—"

"Louise Falmer, will you stop talking for one minute and fetch our guest a drink?"

"Fine, but I want to hear all about it."

I get the feeling that one drink could easily turn into another meal and Lou, for one, would be happy if I spent the rest of the evening here, if not longer. Fortunately, I have a valid excuse to extricate myself.

"Thank you for the offer," I say, genuinely meaning it. "But actually, I should head back to my place. I have some tidying to do."

"Tidying? What sort of tidying?" Lou asks. "You haven't even been here a day. It can't have got that bad yet."

"Let's just say it's something to do with caged-wolf syndrome."

CHAPTER 16

CLEARING up the mess from my earlier pillow-shredding episode is easier said than done, and I quickly decide to defer it and have another quick look through my father's diaries, instead. This turns into several hours. It's the images I love so much and focus on, the drawings, none of which seem to bear any correlation to the words next to them. Trees feature heavily. Ones with wide trunks or cascading branches and leaves. Some of them are scribblings of buildings or parts of buildings. Doors, window frames. Then there are some even more random things. Like a small bed or a cat with only one eye or the picture of a well with something draped over it.

I've already picked up the next book, when I realise the significance of what I've just seen. A well with something draped over it! Dropping to my hands and knees, I scrabble around on the floor, trying to find the diary I cast aside only moments ago. If only I'd taken note of the year.

I finally locate it.

"Shit!" I mutter, quickly followed by, "Holy crap!" It could be any well—they're all fairly standard, after all—but my gut is telling me it's not. It's this well. The one here. And the item laid across it is clearly a piece of clothing, a dress or a shirt, and it hits me: he came here. To the village. To the werewolf camp. My heart is drumming.

Remembering something else, I pick up another

book. There was a bed in one of them, and now that I come to think of it ...

This takes less time to find, and the moment I flip open the page, I see I was right. It's another pencil sketch. A small bed, with a window above. Exactly like the one in this room.

The realisation leaves me breathless. Lowering the book, I close my eyes and try to steady the whirring in my head.

So, he was here. And not just at the camp, but in this room, the one that Freya put me in herself. That must have been deliberate. Yet it would seem reckless to place me in the very cabin where my dad had once been, along with his diaries. Unless she thought it was safe, having removed the ones that mentioned her; but she didn't look closely enough to spot these sketches, these little breadcrumbs of information.

As the moon shines brighter through the windows, I go back again through the notebooks, this time scanning just the pictures, hoping to find some more references to this place. But if there are any, I don't find them. There are a few distinct-looking trees, doors and windows, which I make a mental note to look out for, but it's too late to start now.

By the time I've finally packed up the boxes again, I realise that I still haven't tackled the mess I created earlier. It must be gone midnight, but I can't avoid the clean-up any longer.

I have never before attempted to round up thousands of small, downy feathers. I try using a dustpan and brush, but they simply fly up into the air and land further away than ever. I feel like Sisyphus, punished by the gods to keep repeating the same action over and over again but making no progress. But rather than spending eternity rolling a boulder up a hill only to have it slip back down each time it nears the summit, my punishment is trying to sweep up all these bloody things.

"You have to be kidding me," I say, on my hundredth attempt and finding I have about ten feathers in the pan, which then waft away before I can reach the bin. "Just go where you're meant to go!"

I'm grinding my teeth at this point, but getting frustrated doesn't help, as the faster I sweep, the higher they fly. After a further ten minutes, there do seem to be slightly fewer on the floor but I'm sure most of those are now in my hair.

"Oh for God's sake," I say, "What the hell is wrong with you?" Then start spluttering, as several end up in my mouth.

"Talking to yourself now? It looks like you need some help."

17

"You're back," I say, stating the obvious.

My breathing becomes shallow, and my heart starts to race. It's only now I see him again that I realise the truth I've been afraid to admit to myself. There was a part of me that thought he wouldn't return, that Freya would convince him to leave me here, or maybe he would be called back to London, or he would simply want done with the hassle of having to deal with me. But he's here, and my first instinct is to drop the dustpan and brush and rush to wrap my arms around him. But I don't. I can't expose myself like that, and I don't want to put him under any pressure, either. We stand there in silence for a moment, just looking at one another, and my heart rate returns to normal.

"It looks like you've had an interesting time," he says, coming over to me and plucking a feather out of my hair. "Do I want to know?"

The momentary touch causes a tingle down my spine.

"Caged-wolf syndrome, apparently," I say, trying to sound as casual as possible.

"That's a thing?"

"Who knew?"

I turn away and cross the room to the sofa, where I attempt to brush up feathers once more. I don't know why I'm feeling like this. He's touched me dozens of times before and it's never had any effect on me. Other than pain, when he's bitten me, obviously. A quick shake of my head, and several flying feathers later, and I'm feeling more normal. Well, normal enough to face him again, at least.

"Rather than just standing there watching me struggle, can't you use some of your vampire super speed to hurry this up?"

"I'm afraid it wouldn't help."

"Funny that—I thought you said you were going to help."

"No, I said it looked like you needed help."

"Great."

His smirk has turned into a full-on smile. Most uncharacteristic. This smiling Calin, even when it's all going to shit, is something I could get used to. He's obviously enjoying seeing me undergo yet another form of torture. I'd leave it like this, just to prove a point, but knowing my luck, I'd end up with a lungful of feathers in my sleep.

Donning the most unimpressed pout I can muster, I drop back onto my knees and continue with the hopeless task. A minute later, he speaks again.

"I don't mean to sound patronising or anything—"

"But I sense you're going to."

The corner of his mouth twists. "I was just going to ask if you'd considered asking someone for a vacuum?"

"A vacuum?" I look up.

"A Hoover? You know. It's a mechanical device. Invented at the turn of the twentieth century. Tends to run on electricity. Would assist you with all—" he sweeps his arm in a circle— "this."

Crap. Damned smart arse. The smirk remains for a moment and I very much want to hit him, but then I realise how weary he looks.

"What happened? I thought you'd be gone longer."

"What happened? Good question." He expels a long sigh.

"You didn't find anything?"

He shakes his head. "It depends on your viewpoint. You could say we found a whole lot of nothing."

I sit down on the sofa now, ignoring the feathers. Whatever happened, Calin doesn't look happy about it.

"What does a whole lot of nothing mean?" I ask.

"It means there were no scents at all. Not of vampire or wolf. Even in the place where they found Alena. Or the bar where I saw the rogue. Nothing that I could pick up on. It was as if they had never been there."

"How is that possible?"

He shrugs which is, yet again, another very un-Calin-like action. I feel there's a lot more he's not saying.

"What is it?" I ask him. "What else is there that you're not telling me?"

CHAPTER 17

He looks away and then back again.

"It's probably nothing," he says.

"You don't really think that. Tell me. Is it to do with Freya? With me? Does the Vampire Council know where I am?"

"No, no. It's not to do with you. Not directly, at least."

Of course, not everything is about me. Why do I have such a hard time realising that?

"Then what is it?"

"I did speak to Polidori last night, from town."

Polidori. Head of the Vampire Council. An immortal being who wants my head on a spike due to my killing Styx and quite a lot of other vampires, too. The thing is, if he finds out that Calin is helping me, he might well want his head, too.

"Did he ask you to go back? Does he need you in London?"

"Actually, he asked me to stay away. Said there had been an 'incident'. That he had a few loose ends to tie up and that he couldn't afford any more disasters. He wants me to remain up here another week or so. See what I can find. Of course, you and I both know what that incident was."

"But that's good, isn't it?" My heart leaps at the thought that Calin doesn't have to leave immediately. "If he hasn't called you back, surely that means he doesn't suspect you of anything or that you're with me."

I watch his Adam's apple rise and fall as he swallows.

"I don't like lying to him, Narissa. A hundred years I've known him, and I've never lied to him before."

In an instant, I'm feeling as shit as it's possible to feel, and my delight at Calin being able to stay close to me has evaporated with the realisation that it might not be what he wants at all.

"I'm so sorry I've put you in this position. If I could—"

"I thought I could rely on everyone on the Council," he cuts in. "Styx was a royal arsehole, but I thought he was safe. I thought he adhered to the rules. To the Blood Pact. That he would try to kill you …"

The words catch in his throat.

"To be fair, I was hunting him first."

I don't know why I'm defending that monster. Calin shakes his head. Clearly there's more worrying him than lying to his boss.

"Styx broke the Blood Pact before that, remember? There was your father and probably countless others before and since. But a member of the Council breaking the rules we fight so hard to keep in place … and if one can do it …" He shakes his head. "And there's something else."

"What?"

He hesitates.

"Polidori didn't want to give me any more information about the 'incident', not even where it had happened. I just don't understand it. He's only ever been open and honest with me. Too honest, sometimes. Why is he playing his cards so close to his chest?"

"He must know you're involved with me."

He shakes his head.

"It's not possible. There are no cameras in the dungeon, or the rest of the building where you were kept. No one who saw us together there is still alive. What else could it be? I didn't go into my building with all the emergency services already there and swarming all over the place. Instead, I went to the hospital and managed to speak with Grey, but he wouldn't have said anything to endanger you. Oh Christ!"

He reaches for the table to hold himself steady. His eyes are wide, and I see his lip trembling.

"What is it Calin? Is there some other way he could know about us?"

There is fear in his eyes. I have never seen this, not even when we were fighting for our lives.

"I saw Jessop. He was the one who told me Grey had been critically injured and was in hospital. He can place me in London when Styx died. And—worse than that—I stupidly asked if he knew where you were. I shouldn't have even been aware you existed."

"And, as Head of Blackwatch, he has a direct line to Polidori," I say, stating the obvious.

We are interrupted by the ringing of his telephone.

"Who is it?" I whisper.

He looks at the screen.

"Jessop."

18

We lock eyes.
The phone continues to ring.
Calin has to answer it.
"Speaker phone," I suggest.
Jessop's voice comes through loud and clear. He doesn't even wait for Calin to say hello.
"Tell me she's safe."
"Sorry, Jessop, is it? Is everything all right? It's the middle of the night."
Calin somehow manages to sound quite relaxed. Jessop just ploughs on.
"I don't know why I didn't make the connection when you spoke to me. I don't know how the hell it took me so long. But with everything that was happening and Grey on the danger list in hospital, I just didn't see the link. Tell me, Calin, is Narissa safe? Is she okay?"
The feathers have settled again, as we stand in frozen silence. There's now no denying the fact that Calin and I

know each other. And Styx being killed by a werewolf in Calin's flat and has brought Jessop to the only available conclusion—it was me. Not only that, but he's worked out Calin knows, too. One phone call from him to Polidori, and I won't be the only one on the run. What we say now is vitally important. Without a word exchanged, I can feel that we are thinking the same thing: this could be some kind of trap. But to not say anything at all would be equally damning.

Calin looks to me for an answer. I offer him a single nod, which he reciprocates before speaking.

"She's safe."

Jessop's sigh of relief rattles down the line.

"Where is she? Are you with her now or can you reach her?" He continues, despite the silence from this end. "It doesn't matter. Just tell her I'm sorry. I'm sorry it took me so long to realise. I'm sorry I didn't know enough to help her. But I would never have risked her safety."

"I'll tell her."

A slight pause follows.

"What happens now? Does the Council have her?" he asks.

Calin looks to me again and I nod once more.

"No," he responds. "No, they don't."

"Well, where is she?" he asks again. "No, forget that. I don't want to know. She should travel north, to Scotland. If you see her, tell her that's where she needs to go, to the Trossachs. There's a wolf pack there I visited a long time ago with her father. It was her mother, Freya's. She was meant to run it one day, but she left it and then ... well

…" He clears his throat before continuing. "Even though *she's* not there, they're Narissa's family. If she tells them who she is, they'll take her in, I'm sure of it, even though Freya's—"

"She's still alive," I blurt out before I can stop myself. "Did you know that? Did you know she was alive?"

"Narissa?" He speaks my name with an audible gasp of relief. "Thank God. I was so worried. When Calin came to me and asked if I had seen you, I wasn't thinking straight. It wasn't until later that I realised—"

"Yes, I know. I heard you. But did you hear me? Did you know my mother was still alive?"

"Freya?"

"Yes, Freya. My mother."

I don't know if the silence indicates shock, or him thinking up an excuse. When he does finally speak, I can hear genuine disbelief in his voice. "No. No, I had no idea. Freya … Wow …"

"That was not exactly my response."

"Have you spoken to Polidori?" Calin comes back into the conversation. "Have you spoken to him in the last two days?"

"He rang me yesterday. Wanted to make sure Grey was okay."

"And is he?" I demand.

"He's on the mend. Look, Calin. I need to know what you want me to do. Have *you* spoken to Polidori? Have you pleaded her case? Said she didn't know what she was? She never knew. I can vouch for that."

"Thank you. I have spoken to him but not about this.

There are issues that need to be considered first. He doesn't even know of my connection with Narissa or that I was in London when Styx was killed."

"I understand. But please keep me in the loop. If it's safe to do so of course."

"We will."

"Anything I can do to help."

"Thank you."

And, just like that, Calin hangs up. My mouth is dry.

"What do we do now?" I ask. "Where do we go from here?"

He moves across and flops down onto the sofa next to me, despite all the feathery debris.

"It's late. You should get some sleep. You must be sure to be on good form tomorrow."

"Tomorrow? What's tomorrow?"

"Ahh, yes, about that. I might have agreed to us having lunch. With Freya."

"You did what?"

19

"You need to cancel."

"It's half-past one in the morning."

"You think I care? You shouldn't have spoken for me. You know how I feel about her."

"Yes, but I also know that this hasn't been easy on her either, Narissa. I don't know Freya well, but from what I've seen, she's a good person who has welcomed you into her pack. Tell me, if the Alpha was someone different, would you have an issue lunching with the person whose hospitality you depend on right now?"

It's a trick question and he knows I know it. But that fact is, she isn't someone different. She's the mother who abandoned me for a better life. Annoyingly, he takes my silence to mean I agree with him.

"Exactly," he says. "Look, it's too late to argue right now. If you don't want to go, you can tell her yourself in the morning, but right now, I need some rest."

Knowing I'm backed into a corner, I'm silently

fuming as he switches off the table lamp and lies down with his back to me. Great, so now if I say no, I'm the one who's being unreasonable. Maybe I'll just say I'm too tired or too stressed, or I've got an allergy to whatever she's cooking.

I find myself staring at Calin as he lies there on the sofa. A chill runs through me. What would have happened if I had simply agreed to him scratching me to deaden the pain, that first time he fed from me? Would either of us have survived it? The thought causes my stomach to churn. On the other hand, if that had happened, Rey would still be alive. Hindsight is twenty-twenty vision, as they say.

Despite the exertions of my run with Chrissie and lack of proper sleep the night before, the birds are awake and singing before I finally drift off. Exhaustion pulls me deeply in but not to a good place, as I relive the scene that haunts my dreams.

Naz! Please help me! Please help me!

Twisting and turning, I watch as bodies swoop in around Rey, shattered glass everywhere. I try to get to her. I must get to her, but I'm being jostled from every side. Pushed back and forth. Shaken so violently it feels like they're trying to rip my shoulders clean off my body.

Naz! Please!

She's a witch. The thing vampires fear more than anything else on the planet. And she's just exposed herself to them to save me. And there's no way I can get to her.

Naz! Naz!

The shaking's so bad now, I can barely keep standing.

"Narissa! Narissa!"

I sit bolt upright, sweat pouring down my back. Blinking, I take a moment to make sense of my surroundings. Outside it's light. Midday-strength light. The dawn chorus has been replaced by the sound of people going about their duties, and yet the echo of that one voice continues to resonate in my mind.

"You're awake," Calin says softly, drawing me further away from those memories of the Blood Bank. "It's all right. You're safe."

His hand reaches out and wipes the sweat from my forehead before he speaks again.

"Styx?" he asks.

I shake my head. "Rey."

He fetches me a glass of water from the sink, which I down without so much as a thank you.

"It was so real," I say eventually. "I could hear her voice."

"I'm sorry," he says. "I wish there were something I could do."

I've always thought it was a trite, simplistic response when people said that. Like the way Jessop did when my dad died, when there was something he could have done. He could have believed me. But he chose not to. With Calin, it's different. I can tell by looking at him, he'd do anything in his power to make this pain go away. Then I remember last night and what he told me he'd agreed to today, which pissed me off more than just a little bit. Which is I why I tilt my head and say, "You could cancel the lunch plans you made with Freya. That would definitely help."

"Nice try," he says, throwing me a grin that lifts my spirits, if only for a moment. "Speaking of which, you'd better get in the shower. I said we'd be there in an hour."

A LITTLE OVER AN HOUR LATER, I'm standing in front of her door. Technically, Calin is in front, as I hang back and let him knock. Eventually, it swings open.

"Sorry. Come in. I'll just be a second," she says, disappearing inside.

"Can I help?" Calin offers.

"No, no. It's fine," she calls back to us. "The gas can be a little temperamental, that's all. Make yourselves at home."

As we hover in the doorway, Calin looks expectantly at me for a signal as to what to do next, to which I respond with a suitably useless shrug. After all, he was the one who agreed to this.

"Please, come in," Freya calls again.

There's only so long I can linger here. Besides, the sooner we've done this, the sooner I can disappear back to my cabin and continue feeling sorry for myself. I force myself to follow him inside.

Everything is open plan. Freya is in the far corner, waving a tea towel at smoke which is billowing around her. I guess you're screwed if you need the fire service all the way out here. Particularly with all the wood around. Although a small house fire would be a suitable excuse to get out of this situation.

A long dining table fills the space in front of the kitchen and to our left is the living area, with a large sofa, a woollen blanket draped over the back of it. A huge bookshelf fills an entire wall, jam packed with volumes arranged haphazardly. Some are stacked horizontally, some vertically, others lie at a slant and there's no apparent order to her collection. She reads a lot then. That shouldn't really be a surprise. It's how I like to spend my time, and it's a habit I definitely didn't get from my dad. I'm intrigued to know what kind of thing she's into. Horror? Crime? Urban Fantasy? I don't get the impression she's a Mills-and-Boon-romance sort of person, but I could be wrong. I'm about to look further when I catch sight of a desk and, more notably, what's on top of it.

A large photo frame has caught my eye, the silver blackened with age. It's far more ornate than anything else in the place and is about the size you'd put a wedding picture in, which brings bile to the back of my throat. Dad only had one of their wedding. A tiny Polaroid of the pair of them laughing. Now, I don't even have that. I don't have any of him at all. Would she do that? Would she keep on display a reminder of someone she had so easily abandoned? Unfortunately, it's at such an angle that I can't see what it holds. As I move towards it, Freya steps in front of me and cuts off my route.

"Sorry," she says, her cheeks flushed and a streak of

soot near her hairline. "The food is almost ready. What can I get you to drink? Narissa? I have some lemonade, made with fresh lemons. Or homemade grape juice?"

"I'll have a beer," I say.

She pouts. "We don't allow newly turned wolves to drink," she says. "Besides, it's only just gone midday."

"You don't allow newly turned wolves in the village either though, do you? Clearly your rules aren't set in stone."

"You're right. But I'm sure I've got some non-alcoholic ones somewhere."

A few minutes later, Calin and I are sitting at the table and I'm holding a dust-coated bottle of warm, non-alcoholic beer that must be at least a decade old. The lemonade she's poured for herself and Calin looks far more appealing. Still, I take a large gulp as my eyes are drawn back to photo frame. I chose the seat that gave me the best chance of seeing what's in it, but I'm too far away for a clear view. All I can tell is that it's a picture of two people. It could be a man and a woman. It could just as easily be two women. Is it of them, or us? That's what I want to know. I suppose it could be someone else altogether. But this is the only one on display in the entire room, which means it must be of some significance. Who's to say she didn't remarry? Or have more children? She would have been young enough when she left me.

"Sorry the food took so long." Freya appears at the table with a large plate in her hand. "The oven was more of a problem than I remember."

Leaning over, she places a plate of meat down in

front of us. Meat. I can't be any more specific than that, as it's charred black. Beside it are some vegetables, boiled to within an inch of their lives, no structural integrity remaining.

"Calin, would you like—"

"No, thank you. The drink is fine for me."

Git. I offer him a look that conveys how I feel. Not only has he dragged me here to suffer her company, but he's not even going to suffer the dreadful food.

"I don't normally cook," she says, taking a seat opposite us and blocking my view of the photo entirely.

"Really," I say. "It isn't obvious."

"I usually head to one of the other houses, or just make myself something quick, like toast. Or eat on the run, so to speak. One day, I'll have time to learn properly. You've eaten with Chrissie, I hear?"

"News travels fast."

"It does. You're lucky. Everyone tries to invite themselves to hers when she's got a roast on. Your dad was always a great cook too. I remember that."

"Glad to know you remember something about him."

My dig about her food may have missed the mark, but I watch her face as the comment about Dad stings. Good. It was meant to. If she was expecting me to be friendly, she's got a very short memory. Once again, I'm here for Calin, not her.

"So, how did you two meet?" she asks, her smile back in place although it's so tight her eyes almost bug.

"We're not dating, Freya. He's a vampire."

Another hit, as I use her name. Who knows, this could be more fun than I expected.

"I'm aware of that, Narissa," she says, slightly frostily. "I was just making conversation, that's all."

"Well, in that case, it's actually quite a funny story. I was a blood donor for him. In fact, one time, he drank so much that I almost died. But I guess that sort of thing happens when you've no parental role models left."

Her nostrils flare as she sucks in a breath.

"We met through Blackwatch," Calin interjects. "When Narissa was involved with them."

"You worked for Blackwatch?" Freya's eyebrows rise. "I wouldn't have expected that. Your father wanted to keep you away from all that."

"Well, he didn't exactly have much say in the matter, being dead and all, did he? Besides, I didn't work for them. I stole from them."

"Stole from them?"

I sense Calin stiffen. I know he's trying to keep the peace, but what is the point? Even if I must stay here, the village is big enough that she and I can avoid each other. Shit, when I lived in my flat in London, I don't think I saw my neighbour once. I wouldn't have even known the place was occupied if it hadn't been for the music thumping through the walls at all hours.

"So, Calin," my mother turns her attention to him instead. "You were born towards the end of the nineteenth century, you said. Were you old enough to fight in the Great War?"

"Yes, in France. I was turned right at the end. If it

had finished just a couple of days earlier, I wouldn't be here with you now."

I put down my fork, which still has no food on it, and turn to him. "Really? I didn't know that."

"You didn't ask," he says, flatly.

The comment is curt and his words minimal. His eyes say it all. He wants me to play nice with my mother. Fine. Biting my tongue, I try to think of something non-confrontational.

"So, Freya." I say, deciding I might as well try to get a little more info on the place. "This village, how long has it been here?"

"How long? Oh, centuries. It's one of the oldest settlements in the country. There were Picts here originally, but they'd left long before the first werewolves arrived from mainland Europe and made it their home. We've been here ever since."

"Wow."

I try to sound interested or impressed when, in reality, I'm neither. Imagine that, putting down roots in the middle of nowhere and never leaving. Never trying to see more of the world. I guess it makes sense if you're being hunted, but I've only been here two days and already it feels claustrophobic.

"And how many people live here?"

"In the village? Four hundred, give or take. We have another fifteen members who prefer to live at the further end of the forest and, currently, twelve at university."

Now that genuinely does take me by surprise.

"University? You're kidding me."

"Of course not. We need qualified people. Doctors, pharmacists, lawyers."

"Lawyers? How often do you need them?"

"Far more often than you'd think. Land disputes arise every few years."

"So, you tell people what subjects to take, depending on the skills you need."

"Of course not. One is studying to be a comic-book illustrator. I can assure you, we have no need for that here."

While attempting to digest what I've just heard, I pick up my fork and stab a carrot. The whole thing is so soft it falls apart. Is that a metaphor for me? I wonder. Diamonds are formed under pressure. Sand is formed by gradual erosion. Which one am I?

"Over four hundred wolves," I say, almost under my breath. "How is it possible you've stayed secret?"

"You say that, sitting right next to a vampire. And they outnumber us at least tenfold. Besides, you asked how many people live here. Not all of them are wolves."

"They're not?"

"No. We have dozens who are not yet old enough for their ceremony. And one or two others who have chosen not to progress, even though the gene runs in their blood."

"They chose not to become wolves but want to remain part of a werewolf community? Why would they do that?"

"Because believe it or not, Narissa, living here is an

incredible experience. You may come to see that yourself one day."

"Even better than staying with your own family?"

There's a thud as she slams her cutlery down on the table. It would seem that last comment was enough to finally get a reaction.

"What do you want, Narissa? What do you hope to get out of this?"

"Me? You're the one trying to play happy families."

"No, I'm not. I'm trying to get to know you. I'm trying to get to know your friend, too. I'm trying to answer your questions. Teach you about your heritage."

"A heritage you cared so little about, you kept it from me entirely. Tell me about that. If it's so special, so sacred, why didn't you let you own daughter know about it? You don't get to have it both ways, Freya. Either I'm special or the pack is. You could have had both. You decided not to and now you want to make it seem like you had no choice. You always had a choice."

My eyes go back to the photo on the desk. The way I see it, there are three options for who's in that photo, and all of them suck. Either it's her and Dad or it's her and me or her and someone else. Whichever, Dad and I were never enough.

"You want to know?" Freya asks, following my line of sight to the frame. "You want to know who's in the picture. Here, take a look."

Pushing herself away from the table, she marches over and plucks it off the desk then returns and slams it down in front of me.

CHAPTER 19

It's a photo of two young women of around the same age. One looks remarkably like me and is undoubtedly Freya, from years ago. The other one I don't recognise at all. A friend then, who's image she obviously values more than one of her own family.

"You want to know, right? You want to know who she is?" she snaps.

"I really don't care."

"That's not true though, is it? So, I'll tell you. That ..." She points to the one who looks like me. "That is me. And that ..." She points to the girl with her, "is Jessica, who I was made to kill when I was only sixteen years old. The first person I murdered because of this pack."

20

There's a stunned silence.

"You're not the only person who's killed someone," I say, quietly.

"No. Calin told me. You've killed vampires. You killed beasts who feed on blood and would have ripped your heart from your chest because of what you are. People who had probably lived at least five times longer than nature intended. That's not the same thing at all. Look at her, Narissa. Does she look like an immortal to you? Does she look like she's lived longer than she wanted to? She hadn't lived a fraction of the life she should have enjoyed. She had it all stretching out in front of her. And I took it from her. I tore her life away."

"Why?" I ask, my voice barely audible.

"Because I was told to. That's it. There was an order, and I had to follow it. That was my life. That was how I lived … until I couldn't anymore. And your father … he got me out. He freed me and he gave me you."

"But you left us."

"Because I hadn't solved the problem, Narissa. I had just run away from it. You were shocked yourself at the number of people living here. Imagine it, Narissa. All those people, trapped in the same world as I had been, in a life where it's acceptable to kill someone just because they break your rules. And having you, having my own child, made it all so clear to me. I had saved myself, but that wasn't my calling. I was meant to save them all."

Tears are building in my eyes. I don't know where they're coming from, but I sure as hell wish they'd fuck off.

"You could have brought me with you."

"No. No, I couldn't, Narissa, and you know that. Back then, it wasn't like it is now. It took more than a decade to get things straight. By the time I knew for certain that it was safe, your dad had passed away. I couldn't do it to you. I saw you at the funeral. So angry, so hurt. I couldn't tell you the truth then. I knew it would break our relationship forever."

"You saw me at the funeral, and even *then* you decided to stay hidden?"

"I decided to keep *you* hidden. Why do you think this photo is here, Narissa? Why is it the only one?"

"How the hell should I know?"

"It shouldn't be difficult to work out—because it reminds me every day that I made the right choice, that you would never be in the position that I was put in. Or that she found herself in. You were safe."

"Safe? A vampire killed Dad. And the funeral was over ten years ago. Ten years!"

"I know that."

For the first time since this began, her head drops just a fraction.

"I wanted to tell you the truth. To get to know you. I even went to London once. Three years ago, now. I decided it was time. But when I found you, you were walking down the street with two friends, and you looked so happy. The three of you, laughing and joking. You had a life. And a good one, from what I could see. I knew, here, you'd always be the daughter of the Alpha. There'd always be a risk to you. You were better off where you were."

"You saw me laughing, so that meant I must have been okay? Is that what you're saying? Right, because you have to be okay if you can smile and laugh. No one ever does that to hide what they're really feeling inside. I walked into a den of vampires, Freya. My best friend died because I didn't have anyone to guide me."

I've heard enough. I stand up and walk to the door but then turn back.

"Just one more question. Did he know? Did Dad know you were still alive?"

She shakes her head, sadly.

"No. Of course not. But …" She hesitates.

"But what?"

She swallows hard and presses her lips together.

"But what, Freya?"

She takes a deep breath.

"He never came here. After I disappeared—'died'—I thought that maybe he'd come up, to tell them what had happened, but he never did, and I really don't know why. Maybe it was too difficult for him. Maybe because he knew how much I'd wanted to get away, or because he feared they would realise the part he'd played in it, he decided against it."

But that's rubbish. He wasn't like her. Dad was no coward.

"I'm done here," I say. "Thanks for the food."

Calin is on his feet.

"I'm sorry Freya, I should go, too."

"You have nothing to apologise for, Calin. I think, as we have already established, I am very much the one at fault. I hope you and I will get a chance to talk some more before you go, though."

"I would like that too."

I have no qualms about not hiding a huff as I march out of the house. Calin is immediately at my side and falls into step with me as Freya's front door clicks shut behind us.

"I will admit that may have been a mistake on my part."

"You think?"

"I know it's difficult. But she only—"

"I do not want to talk about her, Calin. I really don't. I want her out of my head."

I stride down the path, past Chrissie's place. Reaching our cabin, I unlock the door, then slam it closed behind us.

"Why don't you go for a run? Maybe that would help."

I'm amazed I don't turn into a wolf there and then and rip his head off.

"Really? After the stunt you pulled arranging that lunch, you're going to tell me what will help me?"

"You're right. What would you like to do?"

The blood is still pounding in my head and the wolf's growling isn't helping. I need a distraction. Something to draw my attention away from Freya and this whole screwed-up situation.

"Tell me something," I say.

"Like what?"

There's a question I want answering, something I've not understood since the first time he fed from me.

"Why won't you feed from my neck? I saw at the Blood Bank that's what vampires prefer. All of them. So why not you? That's what I want to know right now."

21

I think it's safe to say that he wasn't expecting that. He stands there, studying me for a moment before sitting down on the sofa. I still haven't asked Chrissy for that Hoover, so it's still covered in feathers.

"It's personal preference," he says, eventually.

"That's bullshit."

He pauses again before dipping his head ever so slightly. I may not know everything about him, certainly not the way he knows everything about me, but I know enough to tell when he's lying to me.

"That's another thing," I say. "You know my whole life now, yet I know almost nothing about you."

"You've never asked."

"Well, I am now."

Is he looking nervous? Maybe he's just contemplating where to start. Or if he's going to begin at all. And so I wait, although that has never been my strong suit.

"Polidori turned you," I say, prompting him. "I know that much, so how about beginning there?"

"I suppose it would be the logical place, although perhaps earlier would make more sense. You heard tonight that I was in the First World War and died a few days before it ended. As I arrived back in England with Polidori, the war was declared over and everyone was celebrating in the street. Not that I got to see any of that. For the longest while, I saw nothing but the inside of his London house."

"He kept you prisoner?"

"No, although I will admit it felt like that at times. It seemed like some kind of torture. But he was just helping me. Teaching me. Training me to learn the limits of my strength. Forcing me to let go of the life I'd had before."

"Was there a wife? Children?"

"Fiancée."

There's the kick. I knew that love was going to be involved somewhere, and a flicker of jealousy sparks within me, before I push it back down. Jealous of someone who's been dead for at least fifty years? Surely, I'm more secure than that. Besides, what's there to be jealous of? Calin and I are only friends, if that. He probably sees me as nothing more than a burden he wants rid of as soon as possible. Still, this image of him with another woman rolls through my head more than once.

"So, Polidori taught you to feed from the wrist," I say, looking for a less emotive topic of conversation.

"No, not exactly. That's something I adopted myself. The memories of those early days are not good. I lost so many things when I became what I am. But the truth is, I would have lost them all anyway: Ruth, my family. Had Polidori not turned me, I would have died in a trench in France and never experienced a single day of the life he gave me. But it was hard to see things so clearly back then. I hated what I was. What I had to do to survive. The neck was, for me, a point of weakness …"

He's insinuating something here, but I need clarification.

"You killed people? You killed them when you fed from them?"

"I did."

My chest aches, whether for me or him I don't know.

"But it wasn't just to do with drinking from the neck, surely? You said it yourself about newly turned vampires: they kill people if they get out of control or when they've had no one to guide them, which clearly wasn't the case for you."

"That's true, but then … To be honest, I prefer not to drink from live donors at all. I rarely do it. The only reason it happens occasionally, is because it's a privilege afforded to Council members, and it would seem ungrateful if I didn't. Once a year, that's what I stick to, as a rule."

My mood lightens by a fraction. When he said he'd fed at the town, I was worried he'd used someone else and I feel relieved, for whatever reason I'm not sure. But then I realise something.

"Only once a year? But you fed from me twice."

"I know."

"Why?"

He bites down on his lip.

"I'm not sure. And for over sixty years, I've been able to control myself. I've never overstepped the mark."

"Except with me." I remember it so clearly, his grip around my wrist getting tighter as he drew more and more blood.

"Except with you."

"Why do you think that was?"

"I don't know."

I move towards him, but he tenses. Something's shifted. Something small, yet profound, and I know he feels it too. He's killed vampires to save me, tried to reconcile my relationship with my mother, and now he's telling me this. The room suddenly feels hot, and this is not due to the afternoon sun coming through the window.

"Narissa, I'm over a hundred years old. This is … This would be … wrong."

"Age wise, it would be pretty much on par with Hugh Hefner and the majority of his wives."

"I'm not sure I should take that as encouragement." He offers a half smile, but it immediately fades. "This is not a good idea."

"Very few of my ideas recently have been."

I move closer. Nervousness radiates from him.

"I'm broken, Narissa," he whispers.

"We both are."

I take another step, and now I'm standing right in front of him. I lower myself to my knees, and with a swift movement, I sweep back my hair, then tip my head, exposing my neck. My heart is pounding, and I can feel the blood pulsing through me. My hands are trembling, my breath is quickening.

"I trust you," I say.

Fear and hunger flash across his face. His eyes move from mine to my neck and back again. In an instant, his fangs are out, white and glistening. I gasp and tense my body, ready for the pain.

"I trust you," I say, again.

He grabs my face and drags me up towards his, but when our eyes are level, he doesn't place his mouth on my neck. Instead, his lips fall hard onto mine.

I don't know where this has come from or why, but as soon as it starts, I know I don't want it to stop. The urgency and force with which he is kissing me feels as if it's been a hundred years in the making. He lifts me up off the ground, as if I weigh no more than the feathers surrounding us and pushes me up against the wall, my legs wrapped around his waist.

"Say if you want me to stop," he whispers, his voice almost a growl.

"No. Whatever you do, don't stop now."

22

Holy crap.

We're tangled up in the bedsheet. My legs are entwined with his, my hair half in my face, half across his. It's fair to say, my pose is lacking somewhat in elegance. But I'm too exhausted to even care. Maybe it was the wolf part of me, or the vampire part of him, but whatever it was, I am going to have much higher standards in the bedroom department from now on.

We barely slept all night. Every time I felt too exhausted to continue, his fingers or tongue would find another part of my body they hadn't explored before. Then he would kiss and stroke and lick it in ways I'm fairly sure humans can't.

The morning sun is breaking through at the edges of the curtains, bringing with it the dawn chorus, equally as loud as London traffic. Calin shifts into the shade. Even without turning to him, I can tell he's looking at me. Last night, I didn't think once about how I looked. It never crossed my mind. (There were a lot of other things going on.) But I'm now aware there's a filament of drool extending between me and my pillow, and I suddenly feel very self-conscious.

"It's unfair," I say, brushing the hair off my face. "You don't even sweat. You look the same as always."

"You still look good." He moves a stray hair out of my eyes before running his finger across my collar bone. I stiffen.

"What's wrong?"

"Nothing. It's just …"

He sits up.

"Just what?"

The relaxed feeling I had earlier is ebbing away and tension is taking its place. It's not that I don't enjoy lying here. I definitely do. But that's the problem. I don't normally stick around for this bit. This is when it's all too easy to slip up and say something stupid or end up agreeing to things like dates or relationships or possibly admitting to feelings you weren't even sure were there in the first place. I clear my throat and sit up as well.

"Why don't you have your bottom fangs?" I ask, shifting the conversation away from me. "It's to do with the Blood Pact, right?"

He pauses, as if he wants to say something else, wants to return to my earlier response but then flops back down onto the bed.

"Yes, it's part of the Blood Pact."

"As a sign? So you can see who has agreed to it?"

"Partially. The bottom fangs also contain venom."

"Like in your nails?"

"Not the same but similar."

I can't help but think that for bodies which are essentially dead, they sure as hell do a lot. Fangs, two types of venom. It's amazing what nature can achieve when it stops having to keep you alive.

"What does this venom do?" I ask.

"It's what we need to turn humans."

"As in turn them into vampires?"

"Exactly."

I feel my eyebrows rise. Until the discussion with Freya and Chrissie on our first night, I'd never really considered whether Calin had the power to turn me. It's certainly never worried me, but I feel it must be a huge part of a vampire's identity. I mean, that's what most of the novels are based on, right? Whether or not they're going to turn the attractive—but ultimately dull—girl into a vampire.

"And you're okay with that?" I ask. "Vampires don't mind?"

"I never had a choice. Polidori removed my fangs before I was even conscious from being turned myself. I've never known anything different to this. That's the way it's done now. And I've never wished I could turn anyone."

"Not even Ruth?"

It's his turn to tense although, in hindsight, talking about his former fiancée when we are naked in bed after hours of what I hope he agrees was pretty fine sex, probably isn't the most sensitive thing I've done. I try to cover my tracks as quickly as possible.

"So, Polidori still has his fangs?"

"He does. He and three other members of the Council. They were founding members. It was agreed that they would keep theirs for the purpose of turning those few selected each decade. The rest of the Council members have been more recently appointed."

"So, that's it? Only three vampires in the world can turn others?"

"That's how it should be, but the world is a big place and there are always the rogues, of course."

"Of course. I forgot those."

This reminder brings a sinking feeling to my gut. There's only so long that Calin can keep lying to Polidori about where he is and what he's doing. At some point, he's going to have to go back to London ... and leave me here. But, for now, I'd rather not think about that.

"Why is Polidori your leader?"

"Our leader?"

"Well, Head of the Vampire Council. You know what I mean. There must be hundreds of vampires who'd like that job and all the power that comes with it."

He laughs softly, before pausing to consider the question.

"Firstly, he's the oldest of us all."

"Really?"

"Yes. He's been around since before any of the others on the Council by quite a long stretch."

"So that's it? He got the job because he was old?"

I've worked in places like that before, where actual ability doesn't seem to be reflected in who gets the promotion. But running a bar and supervising the vampire world are probably different in terms of job spec.

"For my kind," he continues, "age is a big deal. Despite potentially being immortal, our life spans are not what you would perhaps expect them to be."

"Why? That makes no sense."

"In the days before the Blood Pact, witches hunted vampires. They went after the oldest and most renowned first, as you would expect. Polidori survived all that. Nowadays, there is nothing more lethal to a vampire than another vampire. The accumulation of wealth and power that has happened over the centuries often results in jealousy and greed. Fights, even to the death. The fact that he has managed to stay immune to all this brings him an awful lot of respect. Then, he was integral in bringing about the free availability of human blood without the danger of exposure. He was the natural choice."

"You have a lot of respect for him yourself, I take it?"

"I do." He rolls over and props himself up on an elbow. "However, I've had enough of talking about me and my kind. I want to talk about you."

"Really? I'm not that interesting."

"You need to start joining in with things here."

"Do I really, though?" I ask, in an uncharacteristically flirty manner. Even after all this talk of ancient vampires, part of me is ready to go again, more so if it avoids further discussion about my situation here. I run a finger down his chest.

"I know it might not be what you want, right now," he says, refusing to be side-tracked. "But you could have a good life here. A safe one."

"Or we could run away? Travel to Europe. Pretend we're normal humans, not some weird, vampire-werewolf partnership."

Couple was the word I nearly said. Couple. But we're not that. Definitely not. We are just two people who had sex. That's all. Shit, it's still seriously weird thinking about the fact I just did that with Calin Sheridan, member of the Vampire Council. How the hell did it happen? Unfortunately, he's still wearing his serious face.

"As tempting as running away sounds, I think it's better we clear your name with Polidori and the Council first, and that may take some time."

"How much?"

"Vampires are immortal. So a while, probably."

I growl, at which he laughs in a way I don't think I've heard before.

"Well, I will think about joining in with things, when you show me how you did that thing with your thumb again."

"Which thing was that?" he grins.

"I think you know which."

I put my hands on his chest, and push him over onto his back, then promptly straddle him. So much for me thinking I needed sleep. What I need is him, again. He must be able to smell it on me. I'm pretty sure hormones are an easy tell for vampires. Not that I care. I go to shift myself lower, but he grabs me by the hips and flips me back onto the bed.

"How about I do that thing again, *after* you've tried to integrate yourself?"

"What? Are you bribing me with sex? Have I somehow slipped into a reverse version of Lysistrata?"

"No, of course not. I'm just saying that maybe your chances of me feeling like doing that *thing* again, would be greatly improved if, I don't know, you went for a run."

"You better not mean with Freya?"

"I don't mind. Why not ask one of the others? Lou or Arthur, was that his name? If you want to integrate yourself, you need to do this. You know you do."

"You think you were that good that you can manipulate me after one night of sex?"

"I don't know," he grins. "Why don't you tell me?"

23

It appears that I can be easily manipulated using sex. Who knew? As I would prefer this to be as painless as possible, Chrissie seems like the best choice. Last time, we fell into sync so easily. Maybe it would be similar with any of them, but I'd rather stick with who I know.

When I knock on her door, however, it's Arthur who opens it. A topless Arthur.

Twenty-four hours ago, I would probably have taken the time to observe this with a little more interest. Toned abs and muscular arms seem to be a werewolf staple—men and women alike—but after last night, there's a lot to compete with.

"Narissa, is everything okay? Lou's out. So's Mum. She's got a meeting. I can take you to her, if you want?"

"No, it's fine. I was wondering ... well, I was actually thinking of going for a run?"

"You want to go for a run? With me?"

His eyes light up with an enthusiasm I hadn't been

expecting, an energy reflective of Lou, who had been my second choice of running partner after Chrissie. I hadn't even considered that both of those could be unavailable.

"Sure," he grins. "When did you want to go?"

I chew over the idea of running with Art. I didn't get a great feeling about him to start with, but he's not done anything since to confirm this. And the sooner I can get back to Calin, the better.

"Is now a possibility?"

The glint in his eyes grows brighter.

"Yeah, sure. Of course. Sure."

He moves to leave the house and is about to pull the door closed when I stop him with a hand on his shoulder.

"Sorry, you don't have a vacuum, do you?"

"A vacuum?"

"Yup. We'll just need to drop that off, first."

"You can't be back this soon," Calin says, standing in the doorway of our cabin.

"I'm not," I reply, the machine behind my back. "Arthur is taking me." I gesture to where he's standing, topless and barefoot and looking every bit the perfect male human specimen.

"Should I be worried?" Calin asks with a smirk.

"You're the one who said I should go for a run with the locals."

"You're right," he replies. "I retract that. I think you

should come back in here and not leave for at least another twelve hours."

"Twelve hours? I thought you were immortal. Why so short a time?"

My cheeks are aching from all the grinning. This is ridiculous, I know it is. A hundred-year-old vampire and a twenty-four-year-old werewolf. It just happens that the combination results in mind-blowing sex. I just wish the damned fluttering would stop in my stomach, because I'm almost positive his vampire ears can hear it. Maybe that's the reason he's smirking at me.

"Well, I didn't want you to be bored while I was gone," I say, bringing my hands around to the front and offering him the vacuum. "So, I got something to keep you busy."

He throws back his head and laughs. "Is this you trying to turn me into some kind of house husband after one night?"

"Well, I'll see how good a job you do at cleaning, and then I'll decide whether you're fit for the post."

Then I stride back to Arthur, where I turn my head and blow Calin a kiss.

AT THE WELL, Arthur and I strip off our clothes before heading into the woods. I try to be as nonchalant as I can, marching with him naked towards the trees, trying to avoid eye contact.

"Where should we run to?" I ask.

While there's a lot to explore, I have a sneaking suspicious that the wolf part of me has already locked in the memories of all the places that Chrissie took me to, and I would like to know where we're aiming for, just in case I lose sight of Art.

"How about we decide in a bit," he replies.

I expect him to say something more, like maybe an initial direction, but in a flash, he's gone, and a wolf is standing in his place. I guess it's a case of following where he goes, then. A deep breath later and I let the wolf take a hold of me, too.

Wow, you do that so easily.

I freeze.

What the hell? I can hear you.

Course you can. You didn't know? his voice comes back, answering a question I very definitely did not ask.

I immediately spring back to human form. Being naked is the least of my worries now, and a moment later, Arthur changes back, too.

"What the hell was that?" I ask, my knees shaking and not in a good way anymore. "You were in my head."

"Obviously. How else would we communicate when we're wolves?"

"But you could hear my thoughts."

"You'll get used to it."

"Get used to it! It's a complete invasion of my personal privacy."

"I guess you've got some things in there you don't want me checking out."

He winks in a manner he must think is amusing, but trust me, nothing about this situation is funny. Finally, his grin drops.

"I guess Mum didn't talk you through this, then?"

"Nope. We just ran. At least, I thought we did."

I suddenly feel very sick. Oh no! What if she was in my head the whole time? What if she was there, listening in to everything I was thinking? What *was* I thinking? I can't remember. At least I hadn't been messing around with Calin back then, but there would have been other things. Things I definitely wouldn't want my mother's Beta knowing.

"Don't worry about Mum," Arthur says, seeming to read my mind even when he's not there in my head. "She's big on privacy, too. Rarely listens in, unless she really needs to. Look, I know it may seem like a bit of an invasion, and I guess it is, but you wanted to go for a run. Besides, if you don't want people in your head, you have to learn to block them. And the only way to learn how to do that, is by being a wolf."

I chew down on my lip, considering this. So that is what they were on about—blocking—and why running with just any wolf could be dangerous to Freya and also to me.

"I promise I won't invade your thoughts at all," he adds. "Not unless you want me to."

"That's not going to happen."

"Somehow I thought you might say that. Come on. Give it a go."

A second later, Arthur's gone again and there's a

mottled-brown wolf in front of me which tilts its head to the side before disappearing into the trees.

Crap.

Having other people in my head is not something I want at any point, but particularly after the night I just spent. Yet I know Calin will be disappointed if I go straight back without even trying. If I'm staying here, then there's no point in kidding myself. I'm going to have to change to a wolf now and then, even if it's just to keep the gnawing in my head at bay. I guess that doesn't leave me much choice. Ten minutes. I could manage that, I decide, as long as Art keeps his promise. If he doesn't, then I am going to let the wolf rip into him like he wouldn't believe.

Against my better judgement, I'm back on four paws and heading after Art's scent.

I knew you'd come around. No need to feel so worried. I told you, I'll stay out of your head.

Despite the fact that you're in there again, already?

This isn't in there, in there. *We're just talking, that's all,* he says, but despite his words, something changes. There's no sound, it's a feeling instead. Arthur's embarrassment rolling through me.

We sense feelings, too?

Despite expecting an immediate response, I get nothing back from him. I wait, but no words come through. Yet again, there's just a sense. A nervousness.

Do we share feelings? I try again.

Is this a direct question? Because I don't want to get into trouble again.

Yes, Arthur, this is a direct question.

Okay, then. Yes, you get feelings too. In fact, that's what you get most of all. You train yourself when you're running as a wolf. You power yourself on emotion. Let the mind go blank. Most of the time, that's the state you're in. Pure emotion, nothing else. When there are large numbers out for a run, you learn pretty quickly to switch off your thoughts, particularly if you're a seventeen-year-old boy who risks exposing all his thoughts and memories to his entire village.

Memories too? You can see my memories now?

I could if I chose to. If you let me.

Images of Calin flash through my mind. Ones I do not want Arthur, or anyone else, to see. And the more I try not to think about them, the more I can't stop them: Calin and me on the bed; on the worktop; Calin's hands ... oh God. I need to shut it off right now, but it's like someone saying to you, "Don't think of an elephant.".

Without waiting another moment, I do the only thing I know will prevent Art seeing into my memories. I change back into human again. My timing is awful. I'm mid-air, jumping over a fallen tree, when the transition starts, and as it ends, I land on it with a thud, grazing my knee.

"Wow, that's one way of keeping things private," Arthur comments, standing beside me with everything on display.

Shielding my eyes, I straighten up, my cheeks starting to burn.

"That's fine for now," he says, with a merciless grin," but if you don't want people to know what's in your head when you're a wolf, learning to block is the only way, or everything in your mind will be up for grabs. Generally speaking, newly turned wolves have a lot of trouble with it. Everyone's different, but for some it can take a couple of months before they achieve it, to some degree at least. The more you practise, the better."

"So, what about you? Can you block everyone you want to? How long have you been a wolf?"

"Me," he offers a nonchalant shrug. "I was changed at the same ceremony as Lou, despite the fact that she's younger than me. It was just my bad luck. When we hold one, we change all the pack members over the ages of sixteen who want to take part. Unfortunately, I was only fifteen on the previous occasion and had to wait until I was nineteen before I got my scratch. I've been a wolf for a nearly three years now. That's pretty young still, in terms of the wolf world, but I'm slowly working my way up."

"So, these ceremonies, they're a big event?"

'Biggest of our lives. As I said, we don't have them ever year here. Lou was literally just sixteen when she first transformed. Some think it's easier that way, that you get the hang of stuff quicker the younger you are. South Pack certainly believe that. Juliette lets them transform as soon as they are old enough to talk."

"Juliette?"

"The Alpha of South Pack. She's your mum's cousin of some sort."

I'm nodding along, but I'm not really paying attention. I'm stuck on something he said earlier.

"You said it's thought to be easier if you turn earlier.

Like Lou did. So, for me, this blocking is going to be tough?"

"Maybe, but then you don't seem to have any problem with transformation. Maybe it's just in your blood."

This doesn't feel good. As far as memories go, I don't have many I'm particularly happy to share. Seeing my dad die, Rey disappearing under a sea of vampires, Styx throwing Oliver against a wall and nearly killing him are things I definitely want to keep to myself. Nor am I happy to give away the personal ones either: me in the foster care system; weeping at my dad's funeral. Arthur and Lou talked about weaknesses before. If the wrong wolf could get into my head, it would find a whole load of ammunition.

"Okay, teach me how to block then," I say. And, just like that, I can see I've made him a very happy wolf.

24

"Let's start with an easy memory. Like what you had for breakfast."

What I had for breakfast? Well, that's easy: Calin, on the sofa, arms pinned up against his head, the pair of us rocking so hard I thought the whole cabin might collapse. Yeah, that's not a great place to start.

"How about when I met your sister? When she dropped all those clothes up to the hut in the woods for me."

I figure that's fairly safe. Nothing too controversial. Thankfully, Art nods in agreement with this idea.

"Okay, here's what's going to happen: when we change, I am going to seek out the memory of you and my sister, and you've got to try to stop me getting to it."

"How?"

"How do you make yourself transform into the wolf? It's just mind over matter."

"Okay." Mind over matter. I can do that.

CHAPTER 24

"Right, let's do it."

I take a deep breath ready to change, before stopping myself.

"Wait. Am I meant to be thinking about it or not? Your sister, that is?"

"It doesn't matter."

"But if I want to block it, does that mean I should or shouldn't think about it? Right now, I'm not sure I can't think about it."

His grin is both annoying and completely unhelpful.

"It's *your* head, I'm afraid. You're going to have to figure it out for yourself."

A split second later, he's a wolf and I'm still wondering if I have any idea of what I'm supposed to do.

"Here goes nothing," I say, and join him.

My first thought is, strangely, whether or not drones ever fly over this place. You know, the type that are used for filming nature programmes. If they do, what would they make of two wolves, just lying in the grass next to each other? I guess that would happen naturally, so maybe it would look all right. As long as they didn't catch us morphing. My train of thought stops suddenly, like I've just been struck by déjà vu, only it's not that. It's something different. Like some new part of my mind has been connected.

God, Lou doesn't stop talking, does she? And how many clothes did she think Narissa needed? Although those ones she came in ... not a good look. Honestly, why Mum trusts her with anything, I do not know.

What? Wait! You can see it? You took that memory from me? How? I thought you were going to give me some time to get ready.

Why did you think that? You weren't concentrating. Your mind was everywhere. Nature documentaries? Really? That's what you think about?

And you said you weren't going to read my thoughts, just my memories.

Sorry about that. I must have forgotten.

A surge of frustration ripples through me. How had I not felt more than just that strange connection? How had I not spotted him rooting around in there? Why had I trusted him to actually help me?

Firstly, you can trust me, because I'm trying to help you. Secondly, it was so easy for me because you don't know what you're feeling for, and you're too easily distracted. Okay, your turn. Find out what I had for breakfast.

What?

Seriously, give it a go.

My frustration is growing rapidly, and I know he can feel it. His nonchalant attitude towards all this doesn't help, either.

I don't know what I'm supposed to do. "Find a memory." That's hardly helpful!

An audible sigh reaches my ears. I didn't know wolves did that.

Think of it like following a path. Your own mental path into my thoughts. The link is already there, otherwise we wouldn't be able to talk like this. So just follow where the words come from and go deeper.

I take a moment to digest what he's said and decide I

like this analogy. It makes sense. The path is already there. So how do I follow it? The words, his inner voice. That's the only thing I've got, so that's what I'm going to have to go with. Follow the line between our voices.

That's it. I can feel you trying to get in.

His words offer all the support I need. I latch onto them. The tone, the timbre, then even more. The feeling behind them, the place that they originate from. A new emotion floods through me: apprehension. But it's not mine; it's his. That's where I am now. I'm in his thoughts. Now breakfast. How do I find that? Search for him in his house, maybe?

It's as if a thousand tendrils of inner light are attempting to connect my mind with his. Searching, scouring, knitting themselves together. Each gives me the tiniest flicker of knowledge, with some areas feeling newer and fresher than others. Breakfast wasn't that long ago, so I find a place that feels relatively new. A pathway that feels fresh.

You didn't eat breakfast. You were going to, but then I turned up.

The apprehension I sensed is replaced with something else. Whilst I don't like to blow my own trumpet, I'm pretty sure he's impressed.

I am. I seriously am. It took me a fair bit longer to do that party trick. Of course, I wasn't trying to block you. I made it easy for you.

By picking a meal you didn't have?

You got there, didn't you?

Yes, I did.

Whether it's foolish or not, I'm starting to feel rather confident. Excited even. This part of being a wolf could be fun, and rooting around in memories is much more entertaining than just listening to people talk.

Okay, I want to see what happens at a ceremony.

Wow, that's a bit of a jump. Okay, but I'm going to put a block up this time. You'll have to get through that, first.

Fine.

I immediately send out those tendrils, back through the connection, but there's a difference now. Last time, it was so straightforward. They could go in any direction they or I chose. Now there are routes that are shut off. No, not shut off, just tougher to get through. Like paths that have run into deep mud or quicksand. It doesn't feel impossible, though, just harder.

Glide through it. I find myself talking to the filaments, like they will somehow understand. *There's nothing to stop you. It's not really a barrier. Don't force yourself, though. Just slide on through.*

The threads pause, hovering, like they don't believe me. He's making it harder, putting up a fight. I can feel it. But I persist and gently coax those tendrils through. I got control of my transformation immediately. I can do the same with this. Besides, we've got plenty of time.

With one more push, I feel the resistance weaken. Then it's just a case of applying more force. I lunge into the block, feeling it yield and then collapse altogether. I'm in. Whatever I want is mine.

Images start flashing in front of me, at speed. It's like a montage of film clips, spinning through my mind.

People. Wolves. Family. Laughter. Yet it all makes sense. I'm at a large gathering. I see Lou, looking ecstatic. But then there's a feeling of overwhelming emotion. Arthur is excited, yet terrified. Desperate to start, yet so uncertain. Frustrated that he's had to wait so long for his birthright. And the weight. The weight of history. Of duty. Of living up to his mother's expectations.

Wow, and I thought you wolves had life easy. That feels shit.

Seen enough?

Sorry. I didn't mean to pry—well I suppose I did. That was the whole point, wasn't it?

I get it. You got those blocks down fast. I guess it's a family trait.

There's an edge to his voice. He's rattled. I don't want to dwell on it. I don't want to even think about it, knowing that he could have access to those thoughts, but I also feel like something's changed. It's as if my breaking down his block has shifted the dynamics between us. Put us on a more level playing field.

Your turn to block, Narissa.

His voice comes through clearly.

And as you got to see my first close encounter with a vampire, I want to see how you got to meet Edward Cullen back there in your cabin.

Please, Calin is far hotter than Edward Cullen could ever be.

Well, at least that answers one question.

I curse myself for letting that slip out. I have to stop these thoughts right now. One of the foster homes I went to was big on meditation. They should have tried this.

Nothing has made me want to empty my head so much before.

Meditation helps, but practice makes perfect.
I thought you were staying out of my mind.
I think you have to work for it now.

This time I'm ready. The moment I feel that click of déjà vu, I push back.

No, you don't.

It's so different now I know what I'm feeling for. It's Arthur's energy, *his* tendrils, trying to needle their way into *my* mind. But I'm not having it. He went for quicksand and mud to stop me. I'm going for a cage, a trap made of rusted iron, with a current of electricity flowing through it. He's probing, but I'm there at every corner. I strengthen the cage, making sure there's no way in, no small gaps. I can feel him weakening. Tiring. He's still going, but he knows he won't win.

Want to stop?
You seem to have got the hang of this remarkably quickly.
I hear it's in my blood.

There's one more push. A surge from every angle, but I snap back with all I've got. And, just like that, the pressure releases.

I drop to my knees in human form. My whole body is covered in sweat and I'm trembling. When I lift my head, he's there, watching me with human eyes.

"A five-minute break and we go again?" I suggest.

25

By the time we finish, every muscle aches and so does my brain. My eyes are throbbing. My back and sides are in spasm, and for reasons I can't explain, my knees and elbows are grazed and hurting like hell. I've never run a marathon and have no intention of ever attempting one, either, but I think training for one and learning to do mental blocks must be pretty similar.

When I finally get back to Calin, I look like I've been swimming. The T-shirt I grabbed from the well is sticking to me, and my hair is plastered across my face.

The moment he looks up from the sofa and sees me, his eyes twinkle.

"Wow, you look ... great."

"Thank you."

"You were gone a long time," he observes.

"Did you miss me?"

"Did you have fun? Did you learn anything?"

A well evaded question. But since I've been dying to tell him what I got up to, I let it go this time.

"I learned lots, actually. Arthur and I did a bit of telepathic communication, and then I learned to put up a block."

"Wolf telepathy? So it really is a thing, then?"

"You knew it was a thing?"

"'Knew' would be rather a strong term. There have always been questions as to how wolves converse. One thought was that they simply do it on a frequency beyond the range of human hearing, like some other animals do. The other possibility was some form of telepathy."

"Definitely telepathy. And it's really freaky, although I picked up blocking quite fast, so that's good. By the end of the session, Arthur couldn't even talk to me, unless I wanted him to."

"And how did he respond to that?"

I grimace a little. There's no denying he was pissed off at how quickly I picked stuff up. I could sense him bristling. But he carried on helping me, anyway. I might not have been sure about him at first, but from what I've seen—and I have seen a fair bit in his head—I'm warming to the guy. Even if he does have some major inferiority issues when it comes to his sister.

"Yeah, I think there was a slight dent in his pride, but I can live with that."

I'm boiling. I peel the T-shirt straight off. This wandering around naked in the woods, complemented by a night of amazing sex, is doing miracles for my body confidence. But when I step towards Calin, he backs away.

"Not that I mean to be rude, but you know you need a shower, right?"

"I do. And I was very much hoping you'd join me. I think I've earned plenty of your attention, don't you?"

I OFTEN FIND the second time with a guy is disappointing. The first time, I'm caught up in the newness of it all. The excitement of something different. After that, things seem to fall flat, if you'll pardon the pun. Even so, seeing a guy for a second night of fun hasn't been unheard of but beyond that ... not so much. However, with Calin ...!

He's already mapped out my body. Learned the places to touch, and how to touch them. He knows when to go at me hard and fast, and when to draw back, slowly teasing me. Tempting me.

At some point, when evening's come, and the sun has set, I hear a chorus of howls from the forest and the wolf in me rises up, yearning to be with them. But then Calin kisses me again, and the wolf is quietened, and all that matters is us.

I'M LYING with my head on his chest as he runs his hands through my hair, in a manner that I would normally hate. Kissing necks, stroking cheeks, even just curling up like this are all clichés that usually have me running straight for the door. It's strange I'm so comfortable. I think it's the absent-mindedness of it all. And the fact that there can be no question of commitment. This is fun, but it's not permanent or even close. There's a good chance, when Calin leaves the village, it'll be the last time I ever see him. Maybe that's the reason I am okay with these moments, want them, even. Because they're not real. They're a temporary aberration, which is all that I can deal with right now.

The shower was short-lived, given that there was barely enough room for me in there, let alone the both of us. So it was back to the bed. My stomach's been growling for the last half an hour, and I know he must be able to hear it, but I really don't want to move from this position.

"Polidori rang earlier when you were out," he says.

I jerk up out of his arms.

"What do you mean Polidori rang? What did he want?"

"He wants me to go back to London. Things have happened that he urgently needs to discuss with me."

"When?"

"Now. Tonight, in fact. He thinks I'm already driving back."

"When were you going to tell me? "

"I'm telling you now. I was waiting for an appropriate moment, but you were rather demanding."

My pulse spikes as I move to sit across him. It's one thing that what's happening between us is temporary but quite another that it's going to end so abruptly.

"Are you worried?" I ask.

"That he knows about us?"

"What will happen if he does?"

"To me, or to you?"

I realise I was only thinking about Calin. It hadn't even crossed my mind to be worried about myself.

"You'll be safe," he says, obviously thinking it's the other way around. "Even if they worked out where you were, they would never try anything here, while you are under pack protection. It would be all-out war. Werewolves versus vampires."

"But vampires have far greater numbers, don't they? That's what Freya said the other night. Tenfold?"

"Numbers aren't everything. Besides, there's the South Pack, down in Dartmoor, too. And think about it. You took out the ones in the dungeon without a second thought, and you'd only just turned. Imagine what you'd be capable of if you'd spent your entire adult life training. There's no chance any vampire would want to go up against someone like that."

So, I'm pretty much safe, but that doesn't answer my original concern.

"What about you? What will Polidori do if he finds out that it was you who rescued me?"

He stares at a spot on the ceiling before finally answering.

"Polidori trusts me. He trusts my judgement. And I trust him, too. He must have his reasons for keeping things to himself at the moment. He probably doesn't want to worry me."

"How much are you going to tell him?"

"The only thing I know for certain is that I'm not going to say anything that puts you at risk, and I'll be back when I can. You do believe me?"

"I do," I say but leave it at that because I'm not sure I trust myself to say more.

26

This is ridiculous. At least the last time he went to leave, I could tell him that I was afraid, worried about what might happen to me in a village full of werewolves, where I knew no one, except my lying mother. But I can't do that now. There are people I can talk to, go to if I need anything.

What the hell is wrong with me? He is well over a hundred years old. Shouldn't I be freaked out by that? Plus, there's the little matter of him being dead. Oh God, of all the messes I've got myself into, this is way up there under Most Disturbing. What doesn't help is that I have no phone and no way of contacting him. Maybe he's glad about that. He's probably got his foot down on the accelerator, racing away from me as fast as possible.

Jesus, when did I become so damned insecure? This must be down to the wolf. Never in my life have I given a flying monkey's what a guy thought of me. Other than my dad, that is. What the hell is going on with me?

Heightened sense of smell and hearing, telepathy and now the hormones of a teenage girl, apparently. Let's hope this is just a transition period and the old me will be back again soon. The old me *has* to be back soon.

A knock on the door stops the stream of questions in my head.

"Narissa, can I come in?"

Oh great, Freya. The last person I want to see.

"I won't stay if you don't want me to," she continues when I don't reply. "I've brought food."

Food. My stomach growls again in response. Arthur invited me to his for something to eat after we finished our training, but I wanted to get straight back to Calin. Now, though, I'd even risk Freya's cooking, I'm that damned hungry. Still, I take my time opening the door.

"Here," she says, handing me a large plate. "And you don't have to worry—I didn't cook this. It's from one of the families."

"Thanks," I say and take the food.

"I see you've started reading your father's diaries," she says, peering around the door that I had planned on shutting straight away. "I'm sorry I didn't leave them with you when he died. I was worried they might contain something that needed to be kept from Blackwatch."

"You mean about you and the pack?"

"They knew about that. But I could never bring myself to read them. I'm glad you are though. That would have made him happy."

I do a mental double take.

"You never opened the boxes?"

"No ... Why?"

The bottom of the plate is starting to burn my fingers, and I should probably put it down, but as the wolf part of me is so good at healing, I figure I can hold on to it a little longer.

"There's nothing in them about how he met you. They stop just before he arrived here and don't start again until he's back in London. I assumed you already knew that. In fact, I thought that you—"

"That I'd taken them out?" She shakes her head. "No, as I said, I never read them. But it doesn't surprise me they're missing. He always said he'd make sure you were protected, that he'd burn them rather than let them fall into the wrong hands."

I'm stunned by this. All those special memories, all those words and lovely pictures nothing more than ash, long since scattered to the four winds.

"It was just fortunate that I had someone in London when I heard about his death, and they were able to get to them before anyone else. Was there something in particular you wanted to know?" Freya asks, a concerned look on her face. "Is it anything I can help with?"

"It doesn't matter."

"It obviously does. I can see that."

Part of me wants to close the door and be left in peace to devour whatever's getting cold on this plate. But, there again, it's not like I'm going anywhere soon.

"I wanted to know about his visit here. How you met. How you ended up ... you know ..."

"Abandoning my birthright? Running away and

starting a family with a man I'd just met, hundreds of miles from my home?"

"Pretty much."

A small smile lifts a corner of her mouth, but it's quickly gone.

"I could tell you now, if you like. If you've got no plans?"

Time passes far quicker than I could have imagined. It's not at all like dinner the night before and not just because the food is so much better. There's no agenda and no accusations are being thrown around. I have the feeling that this is a story she's wanted to share but not been able to tell anyone before.

"He was so certain it would work. I was absolutely terrified that the pack would come after us and we would be caught."

"But they didn't?"

"They thought I was dead. I nearly did die."

"How? What happened?"

"The plan was to leave evidence that I had been attacked and killed. In the execution, it became a little more authentic than we had intended. But that is a story for another time. Would you mind if I go and get something?" She suddenly stands up. "I've just been reminded of it. I think you might like it."

"Okay."

She leaves me alone, and I review the situation. Tonight, conversation has flowed so easily for the most part. There have been odd moments, small blips, but they quickly passed. I can't deny any more that there's a connection between us. There are similarities in our mannerisms and the way we speak, the way we listen. But does that make things any better? I'm not sure.

Time passes and I think that maybe she's changed her mind and isn't coming back at all, when there's a brief tap at the door and it swings open again.

"Sorry. It took me a little while to find it."

Holding something large and rectangular, she comes over and sits on the floor. I quickly drop down next to her.

"This is the map your father and I used, with all the special places in the forest around the village marked."

It's an old Ordnance Survey plan. The edges are dog-eared and yellow. As she unfolds it, I spot several scribblings.

"For example," she points to a small heart in blue biro, "this is where he first kissed me, and he wanted to mark the spot, so we'd never forget it. Of course, at the time, I was furious with him. Not for marking the map but for the kiss."

"Why?"

"Why? We were being stupid and reckless. But we were so very lucky for all the years we had together—and for having you. When I returned here years later, I would spend my evenings just staring at those two squares, trying to remember it all."

"Two squares?"

She points to the top left corner, where a road is marked with a small star.

"This is where my life started. This is where he met me and carried me to his car and then drove and drove. I used to go back, often. Perhaps, one day, we could go together. It's not much to look at, little more than a track, but I'd like to take you there. Tomorrow, perhaps, if you don't have anything already arranged?"

I feel for her. This is obviously something she wants to do with me, but after the mindfuck it was having Arthur in my head today, I don't think I can deal with her. Fortunately, I don't have to lie.

"I'm sorry. I actually do have plans ..."

27

Calin.

It's gone midnight when I arrive back in London. My apartment smells of fresh plaster and paint. Even though the whole place has obviously been aired, it would be bad enough for a human nose. As far as I can tell, everything has been replaced exactly as it would have been before the "incident". The sofa, the table, everything is in order. Well, almost everything. On the shelf, my bottle of Macallan Number Six—which was previously less than a third full—has been replaced with an unopened bottle. Propped up against it is a note. *I will explain at the Council meeting. Come early.*

There's no signature. There doesn't need to be. I'd recognise Polidori's hand anywhere. I'd expected this. Of course, he wants to talk to me; a vampire was ripped to shreds in my apartment. Now I've just got to work out what to say to him. Normal Council meetings begin at 01:30, giving members the chance to feed before or after or both, depending on their preference. I'll have to leave soon. However, I need a shower first.

Steaming water runs down my back and shoulders, rinsing off the scent of her from my skin. I need to ensure it's gone completely, that there's not a single trace of Narissa's aroma anywhere on me. They'll have smelt it here. And again, in the dungeon, when she changed back to human form. The last thing I need is them jumping to conclusions. Then again, I'd probably deserve it. After all, what the hell was I thinking? I don't mean about breaking her out. That was the right decision. Angry vampires have a nasty habit of killing first, asking questions later. There was no way Polidori would have listened to me long enough for me to save Narissa's life, not after she'd killed Styx. I suppose that should somehow be a comfort. He'd react the same if it had been me dispatched. No, I made the right decision there, and as long as he's willing to listen to me now, I'll be able to explain that.

The problem is what's happened to me. A hundred years of restraint. A century of abiding by all the rules, then she lies her way into my life and what comes next … it's like I became a different person, a reckless one. She spoke of the wolf, gnawing away at the back of her mind, trying to take over. Something seems to be doing that to me. When she is near, I want to *live* this life, not just exist in it.

Even now, I can't stop replaying the images. The

sounds. The feeling of her legs wrapped around me, as I hold her against the wall. Her body convulsing against mine, head back, neck exposed, blood pumping so fiercely. The fact that I could have so easily sunk my teeth into her in the heat of the moment, scares me even more. Sex with a human is only ever used as foreplay to the main event. The appetiser before the feeding begins. But that—what we were doing—was a long, long way from a mere aperitif. Maybe it's the wolf in her that's having this effect on me, is the reason why I didn't want to stop, why I get such adrenaline surges just being close to her.

Hopefully, the distance now between us will help cool things off. And I have plenty to keep my mind occupied.

THE COUNCIL MEETS in the same building as the dungeon from which I freed Narissa. Freed her by killing my own kind. As I walk along the corridors, I try not to think of the dozen vampires lying limp on the floor, necks snapped, bodies torn to pieces in our rampage. I realise how hard the task is that lies ahead of me. All the blame will be placed on her. What are the chances that Polidori will be ready to listen to me for long enough to hear about Styx's part in it all? How he murdered her father. How he lured her into a trap and has probably killed many others, too. Not that I have anyone to support this. The only witness is hundreds of miles away and would be destroyed the moment she set foot in here.

My confidence is waning. All I can do is listen to him and try to read him. I hope like hell I don't have to lie. He would see through that in an instant.

When I reach the door, I am experiencing the closest to human panic I've known in a century. Only time will tell.

Whist knocking is customary, waiting for admission is not. Still, I linger momentarily before opening the door to the chamber and stepping inside.

Polidori is the only one present. He stands facing a bookshelf, his back to me, even though he will have heard my knock, not to mention my footsteps long before I even reached the room. *Don't lie.* That's the thought going around in my head. I'll be safe if I just stick to the truth.

"Calin." He smiles as he turns to face me, although it's fleeting. "Please, sit down. You must have questions. You've been to your apartment, I assume?"

"I have." A small truth to begin with.

"Yes, I'm sorry. I hope you found all as it should be. I'm afraid there was some unfortunate business there while you were away."

He picks up a glass from the table before him. His fingers grip the stem as he takes a mouthful of blood. He seems tense. Angry even. These are not emotions I am used to seeing in him. Polidori is the most collected of us all. The most good-natured. The most, dare I say it, human. He had already integrated himself into the world before the Blood Pact and was paramount in bringing it about. But as sympathetic as he is, immortals are capable of holding a grudge for a very long time. Something is going on here. The rigidity of his muscles and the tightness around his jaw are unfamiliar. Right now, I don't know how I could even broach the subject of Narissa. All I can do is wait for him to lead the conversation, which he does.

"Tell me. You said you were concerned with the killings up north. In what way?"

"The killings up north? Yes, of course."

It is certainly not the question I had expected to start with, particularly following on from the mention of my apartment. At least it's another I can answer truthfully. I haven't told him about the incident with the rogue. I clear my throat but quickly regret it. That didn't sound at all natural. Fortunately, Polidori shows nothing but patient expectation.

"The first rogue was terrified," I say. "Scared enough to tear out her own heart."

An eyebrow arches upwards.

"The *first* rogue—as in the one you went to deal with, what, a fortnight ago? You didn't think to mention this at the time?"

"I didn't. Yes, it was peculiar, but you know how unpredictable they can be, and I thought the matter was dealt with. It was only when the killings continued that I realised it may have been more significant than I had first believed."

He slowly nods, which is good. He hasn't been able to catch me in a lie yet and respects discretion and people taking their time to get their facts straight. But I don't think that mentioning I went for a midnight stroll with an alpha would be the wisest path to take next.

"And what do you think now?" he asks.

"Now? The fact that I couldn't find any trace of this second rogue is concerning. I rendezvoused with Blackwatch up there and they are positive that there were over half a dozen vampire killings in the week between the first rogue dying and my return to Scotland."

"You spoke with Blackwatch?"

"Of course."

"And they could offer no further details?"

"No, none and the way the perpetrator, or perpetrators, disappeared immediately afterwards is ... unnerving. It could be an older rogue we're dealing with here, one who's perhaps deliberately turning vampires."

Once again, he offers nothing but a slow nod. There's silence and I don't feel in a position to say more. The less the better, in fact. There's still the issue of Styx's death in my apartment, and I'm sure he's going to want to get back to that.

He looks up.

"Calin were you aware that the Northern Wolf Pack is very close to where you were?"

Possibly the worst question he could have asked. No lying, I remind myself, though how I'm going to explain my knowledge of them is another matter.

"Yes, I was. Why?"

"Oh, you were. How?"

"I ran into one of their members when I was tracking a rogue up there years ago,"

"Hmm." A minimal response I wish I could interpret.

"My apartment?" I ask, trying to turn the conversation onto a different path and regain control of it.

I detect his fangs grinding together. He reaches for his drink again.

"While you were away, Damien Styx was murdered … by a werewolf … in your apartment." He pauses. I remain silent. "That was the cause of the redecoration, I'm afraid. You will understand, it was a messy affair. I'm just wondering if you can shed any light on the matter."

"Shed light? How, exactly?"

"Is there any reason you can think of why Damien would have been there in the first place? From what I recall, you two were never close."

"No, we weren't," I agree. "Although I did invite him for a drink last week. As fellow Council members, I thought it was time we became better acquainted. But he would have known I was away. He was at the meeting when you instructed me to head straight back to Scotland."

We both know this is the case, but it's worth restating.

"Yes, I do recall that. Then you had made no arrangement for him to be there in your absence?"

"Arrangement? What do you mean?"

He changes tack.

"This is a very difficult time. What with a witch turning up at the Blood Bank and now this, I wonder if forces are conspiring to make a move against us?"

"A move? Has something else happened?"

"Does there need to have been? Surely this is enough of a warning?"

"In what way?"

He presses his lips together.

"You were lucky. I turned you after the Blood Pact. Those of us who were around before that remember what dark times they were, Calin. For vampires and humans alike. The witches. Oh, the trouble they caused, for both sides, believe me. I'd like to think that these are unrelated incidents, but in truth, I think that would be a naïve conclusion to draw. I'm hoping for the best but must prepare for the worst. I sense a war is brewing."

Whatever I had imagined, it was not this. Polidori fearing the Blood Pact itself was on the verge of crumbling. It's time to ask the dangerous question that has been on the tip of my tongue.

"What happened to the wolf that killed Styx?"

"We captured her initially, but she somehow managed to escape." He pauses and holds my gaze.

"Was anyone else hurt?" I ask, and I'm certain he can sense that I'm holding something back.

"Yes. We lost some good people."

"Have you reached out to the wolves? Have you confronted them?"

"What would be the point? You know what pack loyalty is. It comes before everything else, even their own common sense. They could have the murderer standing right in their midst, and they would still lie to my face and plead their ignorance. They do not trust us. And I'm starting feel I was wrong to trust them. Wrong to let them remain unmonitored for so long. And most definitely wrong to allow them our venom for their ceremonies. They should have been eradicated, long ago."

"What have Blackwatch said about the matter?"

"They will cooperate."

A loud knock reverberates through the room before he can elaborate. I was so engrossed in the conversation that I didn't even notice anyone approaching. Two vampires enter without waiting for a response. A male, with harsh, boxy features and hair slicked back as if it were the twenties, enters first. At his side is a woman, half a foot taller and dressed in a navy, satin suit. I don't recognise either of them.

"I'm sorry," I say, standing up as if preparing to leave. "I thought the Council was meeting tonight."

"It is. There are a few new members."

28

Narissa

"This is going to be trickier with two of us here," Arthur warns, "and Lou can be pretty determined when it comes to getting through blocks."

What he means to say is that I'm better than him, but Lou will be more of a challenge.

"At the same time?"

"Hmmm, we'll see."

Sibling rivalry is actually making me even more excited about what's coming. Waking up without Calin was odd. How could a bed so quickly seem empty with just one person in it? Or rather, how did I so quickly get used to sharing it? The fact that he's gone is a good thing, I repeatedly tell myself. No distractions, nothing to get back to the cabin for, just a full day of working on my freaky wolf abilities. And this time, Arthur's raised the bar by bringing Lou. The only downside is that it's early. Super early and basically dark. Apparently, some of the pack will still be out, but they tend to be the ones who like to keep to themselves, which is what we need.

"We won't try to get into your head to start with," he says. "Just see if you can isolate one of us to talk to, basically ignoring the other one."

"Which should be a piece of cake, as Art never says anything worth listening to anyway," Lou scoffs.

I laugh. I like this pair and their ease and confidence in who they are and what they can do. I guess it's possible to grow up like that when you know you're loved, as they so obviously are.

"All right. We'll run to the clearing first," Art says, "and we'll stay out of your head until we get there. Right, Lou?"

"You're giving me orders? Really?"

She raises an eyebrow, and he offers her a look, which I'm pretty sure is how most big brothers are with their sisters half the time. Her eyebrow drops.

"Fine, we'll stay out of your head until we're in the clearing. Then it's your job to talk to just one of us. Don't worry if it takes a while. We've got nothing planned for today. But remember, if you sense another wolf coming, just change back to human, so they can't get in your head and endanger your mum. Random changing from wolf to human's completely normal when you're newly turned, so no one would find that suspicious."

I know the way to the clearing now without even

having to smell it out or follow the others. My feet take me as if they've travelled this route every day of their lives, much the way they did when I was getting the tube to go to work at Joe's or was walking to Oliver's place. My mind switches off completely. I wish I could say I hate this, that I'm disgusted by what I am, but the more I do it, the more I feel like this is what I've been waiting for. But I still can't picture myself staying in this life.

I step out into the clearing, where Art and Lou are already waiting.

You need to work on your fitness, Lou tells me.

Lou—

What? She does.

Considering how I used to consider just climbing two flights of stairs at a time strenuous exercise, I've been more than a little impressed with my wolf stamina. Obviously, it's not as remarkable as I thought.

You can work on it, Lou says, and I immediately put up a block. I'd forgotten to do that. As much as I like the running part of being a wolf, this mind-reading is more than a tad irritating.

That's better, Lou comments. *Obviously, I could still get through if I wanted, but sometimes putting up a block, no matter how weak, is enough. Any respectful wolf knows that there are things you want to keep hidden, and they won't press if they see you've tried to block it. It doesn't change the fact that you need to work on your fitness, though. But Arthur's right, for once. In your current situation, mastering your mind should probably be your priority. Now, hold a conversation with Arthur and don't let me hear what's being said.*

Arthur's in agreement, or at least there's the sense that he is. There's also another feeling in there, a nervousness.

So how do I do this? I ask him. *How do I talk to you, yet block her out?*

It's all linked to what we did yesterday. You've got to feel if she's there, find the pathway to her. And then not let her take it.

But it's harder now that there's more than one person, because you've got to know where all the intrusive thoughts are coming from. As I try to figure out what to do, something hits me. Rather than just shutting *one* of them out, maybe it'll be easier to shut them both out and then let one back in. With that in mind I put up the strongest block I've managed so far. Now they are both outside my mind, I think through my next action.

Before she died, I remember Rey talking to me once about how she thought magic worked. It was all her own speculation, of course. She'd been abandoned as a baby and never knew she was a witch, until a mishap during a Blackwatch get-together led to her revealing herself and then being thrown out of the job she loved so much. She then had to go on the run, in case the vampires got to hear about it and came after her. Unfortunately, she later decided to risk coming back to London … to me …

I shake those images away. They're not what I need. What I'm trying to remember is her theory on how magic works. She talked about the way some animals can detect and use things we're not even aware of. Like sharks sensing electric fields and some birds magnetic fields or UV light and other weird stuff like that. And then I realise. I can't read all the pathways, but I don't have to. I just need to feel the strength of the fields around me and control my own. I'm no different to Rey, in that way.

So, how long did it take for you to get the hang of this? I say, and I know I'm only talking to Arthur. Lou's distant from me now, all her feelings, her bubbly energy, just a haze.

Not this fast, that's for sure. A couple of weeks, maybe, which is about average, I suppose.

And what about Lou, how long did it take her?

As I mention her name, I feel a slight vibration in my head as if someone's asking to be let in on the conversation.

Let her in. Ask her yourself.

It takes a moment to work out where and how to drop my field, but when I do, her thoughts come bouncing into my brain, like a rabbit on a sugar high.

OMG!!! That was amazing! That was so amazing! I couldn't get in. You know that, right? Wow! You were blocking me out. You know Arthur couldn't manage that until about two months ago.

What?

I turn my thoughts to Art and feel a rush of embarrassment flood through from him.

Lou is very strong at this part of being a wolf. She seems to forget that there are other parts too.

Wow, the jealously is so strong. I don't believe I didn't pick up on it before, and I can't help wondering what's at the root of it. I've never had a sibling, but I know enough to realise this is more than just standard rivalry.

I'm still wondering what the issue is, when my mind starts to move a little like it's in quicksand, and I'm going someplace deeper. Then I realise that Art is trying to block me, and I'm still trying to get in. Shit. What did they just say about being respectful?

Sending him my apologies, I retreat into my own mind. Tension ripples between the three of us.

So how does this pack thing work? I ask, trying to move things along. *Is it like the army? Does everyone have a rank? How's it determined?*

From the prickling sensation I'm now getting, I guess I haven't picked the best question to ask, but it doesn't take long for Lou to reply.

Bluntly put, yes, as soon as you turn and you've mastered the basics, you're part of the pack. You're in the hierarchy. But it's tricky to explain how it's determined. Mental strength definitely plays a large part. You can't climb up through the ranks—if you want to call it that—if you can't block and isolate people. Or read them, either.

But strength also matters, Arthur joins in, and I'm grateful. I was worried he wasn't going to speak again.

Think Scar from the Lion King.

The Lion King, really?

He was clearly the most intelligent of the pride, but that wasn't enough. If push comes to shove and you want to be the leader, you'd have to be able to hold your own against any other wolf. You'd have to be able to defeat the Alpha.

A good leader wouldn't have to resort to fighting, though, Lou contradicts.

This obviously isn't the first time they've had this argument.

There are a hundred other things, too, she continues. *Impor-*

tant nuances. *Take our village doctor. He's really well trained, very well respected and considered not far below Mum, in terms of position, but he hardly ever changes to a wolf. I don't think he's ever been involved in a fight. And he's such an open book. He really doesn't care if people know what he's thinking. Theoretically, he should be lower than even Arthur, but he's not.*

Do you mean Arthur's lower than you? I ask, which is immediately followed by a burst of defensiveness from the elder sibling.

Today, she's higher. But yesterday, I was. And when I take a chunk out of her hide later, for being such a shit, it'll knock her down a peg or two.

It's that fluid?

It is.

And it's also self-determined, to some extent. One of the other wolves, Adam, is a great leader. He's strong, too, and everyone trusts him. He could have stepped up to Beta by now, but he's young and doesn't want that responsibility yet nor does he want to cause any friction.

Then how do you know where everyone stands?

Keeping track of this is difficult enough without adding in the factor that it can all shift on a daily basis.

You just know, Lou says. *You can get lone wolves, too. We used to have a few, apparently, but since Freya took over, everyone's happy to be part of the pack. It's better like that anyway, safer.*

Safer?

That's just a matter of opinion. Art joins in. *Being a lone wolf comes with independence. You don't have to answer to all the endless requests. And you get your own headspace.*

When has independence ever been a good thing for wolves? Lou butts straight back in. *They don't have pack protection. There'd be nothing to stop us from helping them of course, but the Alpha couldn't order it. Now, we've wasted far too much time chatting. Narissa may have managed to simultaneously block the two of us from entering her thoughts, but we're going to have some real fun ...*

29

"I don't think I'm going to manage this."

"Of course you are. I wouldn't have risked it, if I didn't think you could."

"But what you said about not being a wolf around anyone except you guys or our mothers? If they manage to get into my head ... If they see that, you know ..."

"They won't," Lou says with absolute certainly. "They're all the same level or lower than Art and me. They changed at the last ceremony, too. Besides, this lot all think Daniel is an arsehole. Come on, it's a numbers challenge. How many can you deal with at one time? How many sets of thoughts? And remember what we said, if there's anything that does make you feel uncomfortable, just turn human. But I don't think you'll need to. You're like some new Eve."

"Eve?"

Their eyes widen.

"Eve. The Mother of Wolves. She was the only

survivor of the first pack, the one that the vampires created. She was freakishly strong and fast, *and* she was saved by Rhett, her vampire lover. It's just like you and Calin. Wow, thinking about it, you guys are so similar it's freaky. Except, obviously, the lovers bit."

I find myself more than a little relieved we're not in wolf form right now.

"And apart from the fact that Eve and Rhett are mythological," Art interrupts. Lou shrugs but remains unperturbed by his attempted put down.

"Mythology usually has a grain of truth at the centre though, doesn't it? A bit like the start of a pearl. Anyway, whether or not it's true, Narissa is going to ace this."

I'm still not convinced. It's midmorning and tangerine hues of sunlight are breaking through the leaves. We've moved location to another clearing. It's not as big as yesterday's which, considering there are a large number of us standing here, seems odd, but Lou and Art were insistent that this was the best place to try this out. So here we are.

"Won't other wolves be out now? Older, more experienced ones?" *Who might want me and my mother gone?* I say to myself.

"That's why we've moved to this side of the forest, where the new wolves normally come to practice. The older ones give it a wide berth. The last thing they want to overhear is a load of teenage angst from stressed-out cubs. But remember what I said about the block. Put it up straight away and if Art or I feel anything wrong, we'll let you know immediately and you change straight back."

I take several deep breaths and attempt to steel myself. The other day, I was fighting to keep Arthur out of my head in a one-on-one with someone who was trying to help me. Now I've got to keep out twenty-odd young wolves, who will all, most probably, have something to prove.

Pairs of yellow eyes gleam out at us from the dense forest. This is it. Time to change. Time to face the music.

"Just concentrate," Lou tells me. "You've got this."

A second later, she's a wolf and I'm wondering what the hell I'm about to step into.

The moment I change, I'm hit by a tsunami of noise and emotions. My block is immediately up, and they can't get into my thoughts, but that doesn't stop theirs from almost overwhelming me. Lou wasn't joking about the teenage angst. I thought I had been bad at their age, but this is insane. I'm immediately feeling everything from unrequited love to embarrassment and shame. A desperate need to fit in is a recurrent theme.

Please don't let me turn human. Please don't let me turn human. Why does it keep happening when I'm stressed? No one else does any more.

Obviously, growing up here doesn't prevent all the usual issues. Then, their thoughts home in on me.

Why are we being told to do this?

Is she single? She looked pretty hot. Nice tits.

Jesus Christ. Less than one minute in and I've heard too much. It's bad enough when you spot guys ogling you when you're fully dressed in a London bar. Hearing these comments, when you're ninety-nine percent certain they've already seen you naked, is not something I can deal with right now. Time to put a stop to this.

Concentrating my mind, I ping my field outwards, covering pervy guy's mind to start with. It feels so natural! I sweep the field wider. One by one, the voices in my head filter out until I'm alone with my own thoughts. Have I done it? It feels like I have. I can't hear anyone, but maybe they've just stopped talking.

I'm just wondering if I should call out to Lou and ask if I've done this right, when something changes. There's been a shift in the pack. I can't say for certain what it is, but it feels as though I've caused it.

I don't have much time to dwell on this as there's a knocking going on in my head. It's Art and Lou, asking to be let back in.

Wow. Okay, that was ... wow ... Mum used to talk about Freya, when she had just turned, you know. They said they'd never seen anything like it. She could have been a beta in just one month. Well, that's what Mum said, at least. I guess she might be a bit biased, but Jesus—

What my sister is trying to say here, Narissa, is that this was seriously impressive work. You're sure you only turned a week ago?

I guess I must have had good teachers, I say and let a little of my pride flow through into them, so they can tell how grateful I am for all their support. *Also, as we're now on telepathic terms, please call me Naz. No one calls me Narissa. No one except—well, you know.*

Naz it is, Lou responds.

It's crazy how I can feel them smiling at me. On the outside, they just look the general level of terrifying that I have always associated with wolves. But, inside, I can sense it.

So, what do I do now? I ask. *Shall I talk to them one by one? Like I did with you two, earlier?*

You could, Lou responds. *Although I don't think it's going to be enough of a challenge. We need to think of something—*

Lou stops, mid-sentence, which is odd for her when she's on a roll, and I suddenly sense fear cascading through her and Art.

What is it? I ask. *What's going on?*

Change! Change now!

30

Lemonade. Chips and gravy. The taste of a Braeburn apple straight from the fridge. Even as I almost taste the food on my tongue, I can feel that something's wrong. I'm not changing. I'm still not human. What's going on? There's a burning pain now in my temples, and someone is using a huge amount of energy to force their way past my block.

When I turn my head, I see a great black wolf padding towards me.

Sorry about my little intrusion. I didn't want you to disappear before we had the chance to chat.

Along with the words in my head, I hear a deep external growl.

Daniel.

I see my reputation precedes me. You were planning on turning human, were you not? I apologise. It's a beta prerogative, to keep wolves from turning when we want to have a conversation with them. Management perks, you might say.

He's a beta? I try to keep my shock to a minimum as I attempt to reinforce my block with all I've got. For some reason, I'd assumed there was only one beta, Chrissie. I sure as hell didn't expect the wolf that was after my mother's throne to be another second in command. I force my fear down and lock eyes on him, but I don't offer him anything. Not a single word. If I get to choose where to direct my thoughts and comments, he is very definitely the last place they're going.

Ah, so you've been training I see, Narissa. Is that right? Narissa of ... where is it you're from again?

My thoughts stumble over each other. Part of me wants to reply. No, that's not right. Part of me feels I must reply. I have to reply. I've put everything I can into my block, but he's still there. I can feel thin tendrils advancing through my barrier. It won't be long until he's in there fully. Until all my thoughts and memories are laid bare.

What are you doing this way, Daniel? Lou speaks up. *Can we help you with something? Did my mother send you?*

No, no. I was just hoping to make introductions, that's all. Although Narissa here seems very guarded. Has she not learnt it's impolite to resist your superiors?

I heard it wasn't polite to try and enter another pack member's mind without their permission. My voice cuts through, and in return I receive a chuckle. But there's no warmth in it.

Are you a member of our pack, then? You do seem to have those privileges. Her protection. She certainly wouldn't want me digging around in your head, would she? Why do you think our beloved

CHAPTER 30

Alpha just accepted you, without a single discussion or consultation? Not even with me, or her other beta. Don't you find that strange?

She's the Alpha, isn't she? I didn't think she had to answer to anyone.

Around me, the rest of the young wolves are shrinking back into the forest, some of them with their tails between their legs. Only Lou and Art remain. Lou's fear is doubling by the second. I feel a slight conflict within Art. For all his usual nervousness, he seems completely collected. Odd that. Maybe he realises that to challenge Daniel in any way would only make things worse. The Beta must know how these two feel about him, but he doesn't seem to care in the slightest. All his attention is on me.

So, tell me, Narissa, how well do you know our dear Freya? The rumour mill is conflicted on the matter.

A growl is rising from the base of my throat. I somehow manage to swallow it back down.

Not well at all. We've barely had three conversations.

He'll be able to detect no lie in my words. It's the truth. Three conversations and only one civil.

But she visited you last night, did she not? Made a personal trip to your cabin.

Great, so he's been spying on me, too.

Yes, she came to tell me some things about your history. About wolves. About Eve and Rhett. It's all very new to me, given that I didn't know werewolves even existed until I became one the other day.

Yes, funny that. Totally naïve, and yet you have no issue

blocking out a whole group of gammas. And doing a pretty good job of resisting even me. Why do you think that is?

Beginner's luck? I offer.

He's prowling around the three of us, corralling us into a tighter group. Soon, we're going to be on top of each other, with no means of escape. The block in my head is continuing to weaken. Even as he talks and paces, I can feel him loosening the knots that hold it together. I don't know how much longer I can maintain it. If only I could just change back to human.

But gammas are not what they used to be. To be honest, I'm not surprised you could do it so easily. With every ceremony since that woman came to power, the new wolves have turned out weaker and weaker. In my day, half of them would have been dealt with before they even got as far as the village. But your ... Freya is too soft. I wonder how you would fair against a real wolf. Someone like me, for instance?

It's not a question, it's a challenge and one I can feel Arthur and Lou are desperate for me not to take. They're not the only ones. My skull is now buzzing with the power of his grip as he tries to wheedle his way in. *Diet Coke*, I say to myself. *Diet Coke. Cider. Black espresso. Cinnamon buns.* Nothing's working.

I'm sorry you were unaware of beta privileges, Narissa, but I have a few things I would very much like to discuss with you.

Then let me change back. We can do that as humans.

So that you can hide things from me? No, I don't think so. Now, where should I start? Somewhere fun. I can't help but feel there's something you're hiding from me. Why don't I have a dig around?

The block is so weak now, it feels like a piece of latex,

stretched and stretched until it's become almost transparent. Any second now, he's going to poke a hole straight through it. But it's not a piece of rubber, I remind myself. It's a field, just like Rey told me. Just like magic. Think of Rey. Think of the field.

His laugh rattles through my mind and my blood turns to ice. He's in then.

Yes, yes, I am. You put up a good fight, for a gamma, that's for sure. Too good, possibly.

I try to ignore him.

Think of the field. Think of the magic.

Magic? Really? How novel. But I'm interested to see who this Rey is. A friend? Someone I can use? Let's have a look, shall we? Wow, a lot of pain around that name. I wonder what that's all about. A girlfriend? A lover? Did she break your heart? I can't wait to see.

Despite the hundreds of memories Rey and I made together, I know there's one he'll home in on. The one of her I see every day and every night, without fail. The one that wakes me up in a cold sweat, and haunts me, even when I'm not asleep. And no one is getting to see that. Especially not him.

A snap of electricity fizzes in the air around me and my block thickens and then does it again and yet again. It is just a field. And I was born to control it.

There's another snap, another fizz, and a yelp rings out. It's from him! From Daniel! I've blocked him! And more than that, I'm in *his* head. I don't know how I can tell, but I am. So much anger, so much pain is flooding through to me. How does someone amass all that? And it's so focused, so directed. I feel my mind being guided through his, taking me to the answer I seek. It's Freya! Everything goes back to Freya. But there's another name in there, too. Whipper.

Who the hell is Whipper?

That's when the pain strikes my side.

31

Daniel was the one who lashed out with a giant wolf paw, so I'm amazed to see him staggering across the clearing, yelping. His pain echoes around my skull but his grip on me has gone, and I know that as soon as I try to change, it's going to work this time.

No sooner have I done that than Art and Lou are standing next to me, also in human form.

"What happened? What did you do?" Lou looks panic-stricken.

"I don't know. I didn't do anything *to* him. I just wouldn't let him reach my memories, that's all. I just blocked him, and then he went for me."

Looking down, I can see a purple bruise blooming beneath my skin. After gingerly prodding around—a cracked rib, at least—I look up just in time to see my friends exchange a worried glance.

"What? I just did what you showed me. You were the ones who taught me how to block."

"Yes …" Art, starts nervously. "To block gammas. New wolves, like yourself. Maybe a few of the weaker older ones, too. But Daniel isn't a gamma. He's a beta."

"Which means what? I'm not allowed to block him?"

"It's not that you're not allowed …"

"Just that you shouldn't be able to. The Alpha and Betas have free rein, not that they often want to peer inside a bunch of gammas' heads."

"But Daniel would definitely have wanted to see into yours."

If possible, Lou's looking even more panicked than she did before.

"Shit. This is … shit," she says.

"Shit in a bad way?"

I realise that the term is not often used as a positive, but I feel it necessary to clarify, just in case.

"This is bad shit," Arthur disappointingly confirms.

"Did he see you and your mum when he was in there? Does he know?"

"I don't think so. He wasn't going after her. He was going after some other memories."

They don't look as relieved as I'd hoped they would.

"There's no way he's going to overlook this," Lou says and bites down on her lip.

"And even if he didn't get all the way into your head, the fact that you managed to do that to him … he's going to arrive at the conclusion that you and Freya are linked. Your bloodline is the only thing that could have been responsible for that little demonstration."

Great. So, in not outing myself, I've outed myself. Just

perfect. That still doesn't answer all my questions, though.

"But why all the yelping and why did he run away? It wasn't like *I* hurt *him*. But he was in pain. I could feel it."

"You were in his head, too?"

"Shit, I'm in trouble, aren't I?"

"You? No way?" Lou shakes her head vehemently. "He's the one in trouble. That's why he scarpered like that. Freya made it clear that you weren't to be touched. And, anyway, dominance fights involving gammas aren't allowed until they have progressed enough to be officially assimilated into the pack. Before that, it's too big a risk. If one accidentally changed back to human without meaning to, well, you can see what would happen."

I can and it isn't pretty. Considering super-strength vampires don't stand a chance against a werewolf, I can imagine the damage that could be done by one to another in human form.

"Even when they're integrated, there's no way a beta should go after a newly turned wolf." Art joins in. "It's just not done. What's the point? A gamma's never any threat to them. That's why he was in such pain, because he went against the Alpha, and it's more than likely that she knows it."

Simply put, if Daniel wasn't an enemy before, he sure as hell is now.

"How do I make this better?"

"I don't think you can," Lou replies, nervously.

"You could always make a play for Beta. Do you see yourself as a leader?"

"That's not helpful, Art."

"I'm not joking."

He looks at me, and I can see he means it.

"You're only a week in, Narissa, and you're this good. This is the stuff of legends. This is the stuff of, well … Freya."

"Brilliant."

Maybe their advice should have included not to stand out so obviously. Unfortunately, it's now too late.

"I thought you said rising up the ranks had to do with physical strength, too."

"You can work on that. And why not go on the attack? If you can get into his head quickly enough, he'll never even have the chance to strike out."

"That's a bloody great *if,* Art," Lou says. "More than likely, she'd be on a suicide mission."

"Then what do I do?"

I wait for them to say something. Anything. Even a sibling dig would be better than this worried silence.

"I think we're going to need some time to figure this out," Art says, eventually.

32

We reach the well, then walk in silence to the village, our minds occupied with what has just happened. How I inadvertently challenged a beta. How I outed myself as daughter of the Alpha. I feel like, maybe, this is something I should talk to Freya about, but considering we've only just managed our first civil conversation, the last thing I want to do is let her know what a liability I have become. Maybe I'll mention something if it comes up when I next see her, although how I expect that to happen, I'm not sure.

As I reach my cabin, Chrissie steps out of hers.

"I wondered what happened to you guys. You've been gone all day. I take it all went well?"

The question is addressed to me, but it's Lou that answers.

"It was certainly interesting," she says.

Chrissie smiles. "Well, get washed up. I thought we'd

have an early dinner. I've made plenty for you too, Narissa, if you'd like to join us?"

I look to Lou and Art for a reaction. Lou's unusual calm has been particularly conspicuous, and the last thing I want to do is make her feel uncomfortable in her own home, but—as I should probably have guessed—she throws me a grin.

"That sounds great. Thank you," I say.

Dinner is a slightly awkward affair. Unlike before, when the air had been full of laughter and playful bickering, Art, Lou and I are notably quiet.

"What's going on with you three?" Chrissie asks, as she watches us pick at our food. "Is this about the funeral?"

"Funeral? What funeral?"

"Alena's of course. I know it's tough, but I think Freya has made the right call. We need to do it soon. It's just a shame."

"What is?" I ask, hoping I don't sound rude. "Why wouldn't you want to do it?"

I look to Chrissie for the answer, but it's Art that replies.

"When a wolf dies, on the day of the next full moon, their body is taken into the forest, where it's cremated. The whole pack attends, standing and watching as humans, until the flesh is ash."

"It can take hours," Lou cuts in. "But everyone waits in silence. Then, when the fire finally goes out, we turn into wolves and howl at the moon. Then, still howling, we run in a circle, faster and faster. There are so many of us thundering around that it sends the ash up into the air."

"It's a spectacular sight," Chrissie says, "everyone running together in perfect unison. The whole earth trembles. I remember every one I've ever attended."

It sounds like something from a nature documentary. Don't whales have a ritual they perform together? Or maybe it's dolphins. I'm not sure. It doesn't seem the most appropriate time to ask.

"Why is there any question about doing it now?" I ask, feeling this isn't insensitive.

"Only the flesh burns," Chrissie answers. "The bones remain. When the ashes have been scattered by the pack, the family members return to human form and commit the bones to the earth."

"And Alena's family are missing," Art interrupts. "Her brother, her sister and her mother. They're all among the missing wolves."

"So, who will look after the bones?"

"This is the dilemma and why so many wolves have an opinion on it. As Alpha, Freya will take one bone, anyway. After that, Alena had a lot of good friends. Esther, Ruth, Adam ... too many to mention, really. But they're friends, not family. And, if Alena's is still alive somewhere, then not waiting for them would be hugely disrespectful. But you could say the same about leaving her unburied, too."

I don't remember much about biology but I'm fairly certain there are hundreds of bones in the human body.

Surely there would be enough to go around. Once again, however, this doesn't seem a polite thing to ask.

"So, when will the cremation take place?" I ask.

"Tomorrow night—the next full moon."

I have another question that follows on from this, one that's almost certainly not an appropriate dinnertime topic. Yet I sense the others are thinking the same thing. Knowing how open this family is, I'm sure that, had I not been here, it would have already been discussed.

"Do you think they are still alive?" I ask.

Lou and Art look to their mother. I was right.

Sitting back in her chair, Chrissie rests her cutlery on her plate and presses her fingertips to her forehead, massaging the area between her brows.

"They're a family I know well. They put the pack before anything else. They wouldn't stay away this long, knowing how we would worry, if there was any way they could make it back."

"But do you think they're alive?"

"Possibly, in one form or another."

It's not a perfect answer, but I know it's the only one I'm going to get.

THE SECONDS TICK BY. Can she sense it? I wonder. Could she tell if one or more of them had died? Maybe I'll ask Lou or Art tomorrow. I feel I have pushed her hospitality as far as I can with my questions. I clear my throat and tuck into my food. We eat the rest of the meal in near silence.

CHAPTER 32

By the time I realise it's already dark and I should think about leaving, conversation has returned to normal. Chrissie took great pleasure in bringing out the family photos: Lou as a toddler, dressed in dungarees and a sun hat, riding around on her tricycle; Art, in fancy dress, as the Lion from the Wizard of Oz.

"Thank you so much for feeding me—again," I say, standing up. Can I help clear up before I get going?"

"Don't be silly," Chrissie says, getting up and kissing me on the cheek. "I know these two will be delighted to do the dishes tonight. The way they talk about you, I'm sure they'd be happy if you moved in with us."

"They'd think twice if they saw how messy I am."

"Well, anytime."

Outside, I instinctively turn towards my cabin, before changing my mind. I'm not ready to go back there yet, where there's nothing for me but memories of my dad and the smell of Calin. I wonder how it went with Polidori and the Council last night. If he had any news, I know he'd get it to me, one way or another. It'll do no good worrying about it.

A run would be a very bad idea, after what happened earlier. So, instead, I settle for a walk. I cross the pathway and head towards the field near the well, without any particular plan in mind. Realising how dark it is, I decide I've left it a bit late and I'm about to head back, when I see her, silhouetted in the moonlight. Even from a distance, I can tell it's her. For a minute, I just stand and watch, expecting her to disappear into the forest or turn around and spot me, but she doesn't do either. Instead, she remains there, motionless. And then, without understanding why, I walk towards her.

33

"Are you going for a run?" I ask.

I didn't think I'd crept up on her. I'd certainly made no attempt to hide my approach at all, but from the way she jumps, I guess she was lost in her own world.

"Narissa? Is everything all right? Do you need something?"

"No, I just saw you and I … I …" What? *You looked sad*, is what I'm thinking, but instead I say, "Chrissie told me about the funeral."

"About the issues it's causing, I assume."

"A little. But they talked about the ceremony, too. It sounds beautiful."

"I hope it will be."

Her eyes return to the woods and there's a wistful look in them. Her expression reminds me of Oliver, after Rey was banished by the Head of Blackwatch and she left in search of others like herself. It's as if she's carrying a huge weight on her shoulders because, somehow, she is at fault. Which is probably why, before I can stop myself, I ask:

"Would you like to go for a run?"

She turns to look at me properly. Her eyes glisten gold, and for a moment, the inner wolf seems to shine out from them.

"I know it won't mean much to you," she says, "but there is nothing I want more."

As I step into the forest and change, my muscles stretch and contort to fit the bones as they morph. Beside me, she is already standing as a wolf. An alpha. In a shaft of light, her white fur glimmers almost luminescent. Her eyes are so fierce, it's as though they're speaking to me. And, even without her voice in my head, I know exactly what they're saying.

Thank you.

The thrill of the race is greater than ever before. Energy seems to flow from the earth straight through my paws. This is different to running with Art or Lou or even Chrissie. I may not know much about my mother's role as Alpha, but I can feel her power buzzing around us.

You're a natural at this, she tells me, as she jumps a fallen tree, throwing a glance over her shoulder to watch me follow. *I knew you would be. Come. There's a clearing up ahead.*

We run side by side now, the wind rushing through our fur. She stays out of my mind until we arrive and are standing together out in the open, as wolves.

This is where I learned your father would be coming to the village and I would be in charge of showing him around. Not that I knew anything about him then, other than he was from Blackwatch.

How long ago was that? I ask. *And how long were you together, before you left us?*

He didn't tell you?

He didn't like to talk about you.

I feel a trickle of shame coming from her, and I find the sensation oddly satisfying. No matter how we are tonight, I want her to be reminded of what she did to him. What she did to us. No sooner have I sensed this than the feeling has gone, replaced by something else. Something stronger and far more powerful that spreads from my mind to my chest, burning and fierce. It takes me a moment to realise what it is. Love.

Yes. Love. I loved him, Narissa. I loved him as I have always loved you. If you want something to take away from this, then choose that, not my shame. Trust me, you'll never need to remind me of that. It's my constant companion.

I can't concentrate on what she's saying, the feeling in my chest is so raw. It's unlike anything I've known before. Extreme love, but mingled with loss, with heartache and so much pain. A pain that exactly mirrors mine in losing Dad and Rey and Oliver. Like it or not, we are more similar than I could ever have imagined.

We should go. Others will be arriving soon to prepare the pyre for Alena. With all that is going on, I am grateful that you will be there tomorrow, Narissa. It will mean a lot to have you by my side.

I don't want to ruin the moment we've just shared, and I can hear the expectation in her voice, but I'm not yet ready to go that far.

I wasn't planning on coming to the funeral. I didn't even know her.

Everyone comes. No matter how long it's been since they first changed. Every member of the pack will be there.

But I'm not.

Her laugh is short. Unexpected.

What do you mean? Of course you are. You always have been, whether you knew it or not.

I feel a new tension growing between us. Those invisible pathways are starting to spark again.

I don't mean to offend you, I really don't, but I never signed up to being part of the pack.

What do you think you've been doing these last couple of days with Art and Lou? With the other gammas?

Learning to be a wolf. I hear the defensive tone, the prickliness in my voice, but I don't care. *I came here because there were no other options for me. Because it wasn't safe for me back home. But Calin's fixing that. He's going to talk to The Head of the Vampire Council, and when everything is straightened out, I'll be going back to London. Back to my life.*

What life?

Sorry?

This is where you are meant to be. It's your birthright. You belong here.

No.

There's a new sensation flowing between us. Fear. And it's coming from her, not me.

You can't just change your mind, Narissa. There would be consequences.

But I didn't get to choose in the first place, so I won't be changing my mind. Everyone else here has had a choice. They decided what they wanted to become, that they wanted to be part of this. I appreciate what you have done, letting me stay here, but I never asked for this. I realise things are different. There's a wolf in me now, but surely, I get some say in the matter?

I suddenly remember what Art and Lou said about my being able to block Daniel, when I shouldn't be able to and realise the significance.

I'm not like Lou and the others. I did not sign up for this and I am not part of this pack, Freya, I state with a new-found determination.

Narissa, please, you don't realise what you're saying.

Pain resonates in her voice and a fear I wouldn't have expected from her.

If you don't want to come to the funeral, that's fine. I give you permission not to attend.

You don't seem to understand. I don't want your permission. I don't need your permission.

Narissa, it's you that doesn't understand.

Yes, I do. I am my own person. I am my own pack.

Don't do this.

There are lone wolves, right? Well then, that's what I am. I'm a lone wolf.

The pain is instant, stabbing and sharp, and causes a howl to echo around my skull. I screw my eyes closed, expecting it to engulf me, but instead it evaporates, and the howling stops, too. I wait for something else to happen. More pain. A flood of anger from Freya. But there's nothing. When I open my eyes again, I see her standing in human form.

It's not until I turn back to human myself that I notice how she's trembling. Her whole body is shaking. For a second, I think it's the cold. But it's not. And now I see the anger in her eyes.

"What have you done, Narissa?" she gasps. "What have you done?"

34

She opens her mouth again, as if to say something else, but a moment passes, and no words escape her lips. When she does finally speak, what comes out are orders.

"Go back to the village. To the cabin. Stay away from the woods and don't speak to anyone."

I'm angry now.

"So, this is what happens when I say something you disagree with. So much for being part of the family."

"Listen to me, Narissa. You don't know what you've done."

"Then why don't you enlighten me?"

I can still feel her pain lingering in my chest, from before she transformed. At least she knows what it feels like when someone cuts you out of their life. I'm about to say this, when I notice she isn't shaking with anger, as I had first thought. She's shaking with fear.

"We'll run back together," she says. "You go in front

of me. Make sure I can see you at all times. When you get to the village, go straight to your cabin. Don't open the door for anyone except me. Do you understand?"

"No, I don't understand at all."

"Please, trust me. You're not safe here now."

Did she hear something I didn't? Vampires, perhaps? I thought this was the safest place I could be. As I'm debating what to say next, she lets out a low, slow breath.

"I need to make some arrangements. Some telephone calls."

The sound of voices cut through her words.

"Damn. The pyre. We need to go now."

She moves to change again, but I grab her hand.

"Are you going to tell me what's going on?"

"Not here. Not now. Please. Move!"

I run back, staying just in front of her, as she instructed. There is no voice in my head, no feelings coming through to me. I guess she got the hint and has stayed out. My thoughts flit between being confused and pissed off. Confused by her sudden hissy fit. Pissed off because I don't know how she could have thought things would have been any different. It's one thing allowing someone to stay with you for a while, but quite another to demand they remain and take on a lifestyle they don't want.

When we reach the well, we dress quickly and silently, before power walking back to the village. Arriving at my cabin, she opens the door for me, before stepping aside.

"Remember, stay indoors. I'll come and see you

tomorrow. It'll take a couple of days to make the arrangements."

"What arrangements?"

She looks quickly over her shoulder then back to me.

"I'll let you know, as soon as it's safe."

And, just like that, she's gone.

I'VE BEEN on my own for over twenty hours now. Normally that wouldn't be much of an issue. There have been plenty of weekends when I didn't leave my flat for an entire day, or longer. I've binge watched TV series, refusing to move from the sofa, to the point where my backside basically becomes glued to it, and the television flashes up a message to check I'm still there. But this is different. This time, I've been told I *can't* leave. Just thinking about the way she spoke to me makes the wolf inside my skull growl. But then I remember how she was. Not angry, but terrified.

My caged-wolf syndrome isn't helped by the fact that it has been a hive of activity all day outside. I hadn't seen this many people since I first arrived. Not that I could actually see them, but I could hear them. The footsteps. The talking. Doors opening and closing, as they prepare for the funeral. And the only thing for me to do is read my dad's diaries which, to be honest, I can't face right now.

A little after five, there's a knock at my door. It's Freya

with a plate of food—the first today. Apparently three meals a day isn't a wolf thing.

"I can't stay," she says. "I need to lead the pack with Alena's body. But I've spoken to people. We will get this sorted soon."

"You mean the fact that you're keeping me prisoner?"

"Please, Narissa. Not today. Not now."

I'm tempted to argue, but then take my first proper look at her. She dressed normally, in jeans and a top, but her hair is swept back behind her neck and knotted in a formal style. She looks older, yet more regal. More alpha-esque. I nod and remain silent.

"I've made some calls. You won't need to stay here much longer, I promise. A few more days, at most. Here." She pushes the plate into my hand. "And lock the door again after me."

With that she leaves, and I'm once again on my own. While I eat, I do return to my father's diaries, pondering over drawings, reading comments. But my mind won't focus and refuses to settle on anything. In the end, I just flop down on the bed.

It doesn't help that I have no way of contacting anyone. Not Oliver. Not Calin. It's not that I'd expect text messages every half hour, but some form of communication would have been nice. Lying on the sheet he and I were tangled up in only days ago, I close my eyes and will myself to fall asleep. That would be one way to pass the time.

I'm woken by howling. Hundreds of voices crying to the moon. I scramble to my feet and head to the door.

Outside, the cold air hits me. Judging by the way the stars are dimming against a fading darkness, I would guess it's early morning. Three o'clock. Four perhaps. So that's how long it took the flames to go out. I had wondered. Now, part of me wishes I could be there.

Standing on the porch of the cabin, I let the world wash over me. The scent of the earth deepens as the morning dew forms on the grass. I don't know how much time passes. Five minutes? Ten? The howls are fading. Fewer and fewer ring out, until only one or two remain. Is that the family? I wonder. Is that how it works? Are they already taking the bones? *Next time I'll go*, I say to myself, then remember I'm not staying.

The last howl fades as the last star dissolves into the lightening sky. A yawn makes my jaws click as I turn back to the cabin, only now remembering Freya's order not to unlock the door, although I can't imagine stepping three feet in front of it really puts me in that much danger.

"Naz?" Art stands on the pathway, dressed only in jeans, with a shadow of stubble darkening his cheeks. Obviously, it's been a long night. "I looked for you tonight. I couldn't find you. Is everything all right?"

"Yeah, everything's fine. I didn't go, that's all."

"Didn't go?" He arches his eyebrow ever so slightly. "It's a pack obligation."

"Well, about that ..." I stop myself. I'm not sure I can put into words what happened with my mother, or if I want to. Thankfully, he doesn't push it.

"You look like you need a run," he says instead.

God, do I need a run! The wolf inside me growls, desperate for me to agree.

"I'm not sure that's a great idea. I was told to stay put."

"Really? If you're worried about any of the others, there's no need. I'm pretty sure I'm the last back. Daniel left hours ago. Never one to hang around at this type of thing."

It's tempting, but it's not only the Daniel issue. There's also the fact that Freya explicitly told me to stay where I am.

"And if you're worried about Freya, don't be," Art says, as if reading my mind. "She's with Alena's friends now. So's my mum. They'll stay there until at least midday, in human form. That's the tradition. Everyone else will be in bed. It's been a long night. What do you say? Half an hour can't hurt, can it?"

35

It's amazing how being a wolf clears my head. The moment I'm changed, a sense of calm washes over me. It helps that there's no one else inside there. No one pressing their thoughts into mine. That doesn't mean I can't feel anything at all, though. I know Art's there. I can sense his presence, but now it's like there's a boundary between us. A wall with a locked door that only I have the key to. After about ten minutes, I decide it might be nice to open up communications for a while.

Wow, you really are on your own now, aren't you? Awe is coming through the link with Art. *That's incredible. Are you going to stay like this, separate?*

I think so. For now.

My words cause a sensation to ripple through him, a nervous excitement that I can't quite read.

This is incredible. Really it is. I knew you were something special. That you wouldn't just conform. So, what do you say, fancy heading towards the clearing?

I should really get back.

How about a race then? To the stream. You win, you can come straight back. I win, then I get to keep you out for a bit longer. It's ages since I've had you to myself like this.

I'm not sure.

Trust me, no one else is out. I'd know if they were. And Freya will be occupied for hours yet.

The wolf in me is definitely satiated for the time being, but I have no idea when my next run will be. And he's right, the only reason I've managed this one is because Freya is still occupied with the funeral. I'm unlikely to get that lucky again. Which means I should probably make the most of it.

A race to the stream it is.

The change in me in just a week is incredible. Five days since my first run in this forest and I can feel the difference. The way my muscles move and respond. The strength and power within them. *A lone wolf.* That title sits well with me. Maybe there's a way I can make this work. That's what I'm thinking as I stretch out to my maximum, trying to keep up with Art.

I have no chance of actually beating him to the stream. I realised that the moment we set off. He may not have my ability in blocking, but his stride is over a foot longer than mine and the way he runs is like his feet don't touch the ground. He just glides effortlessly along.

The stream comes up on us quickly although, like most things, I smell it before I see it. As I catch the scent of the fresh water, something else joins it, an aroma, faint yet instantly recognisable. It causes my hackles to rise.

CHAPTER 35

Art, wait, I call out, but I see he's already stopped ahead of me. *We need to go back to the village, now. Fast. It's Daniel. I can smell him.*

I know.

I wait for him to make the first move. To double back on himself towards me. But he doesn't. He just turns to face me.

I'm sorry, Narissa. But this is how it has to be.

36

What I'm seeing, what I'm hearing, doesn't make sense. Art is standing motionless in front of me, and with every passing second, the scent of Daniel is getting stronger.

Art, what are you doing? You know how Daniel feels about me.

I do. And I'm sorry, but this was the only way. It was always going to happen, sooner or later, but this way, I get to keep her safe.

What are you talking about?

He couldn't touch you. Not while you were part of the pack.

The sinking feeling in my stomach multiplies by a thousand. I don't know if it's even possible for a wolf to throw up, but that's how I'm feeling. Sick and dizzy with confusion. A low growl comes from the foliage. Shivers run up and down my spine.

We meet again, Narissa.

Daniel's voice is like a blade through my head, scratching at the inside of my skull.

Although, under very different circumstances. I have to say, I'm most pleased by the turn of events.

The wolf part of me is whimpering, but why should I be more fearful than I was before? Before, he was my Beta. My superior. Now, now he's nothing to me. I could change to human this instant if I wanted to. I know he's not got the power to stop me from doing that. So why don't I? I cast my thoughts out to hear his.

I expect you're weighing up your options, aren't you? His voice brings on a new wave of nausea. *Trying to figure a way out of your conundrum. Well, there's not one, I'm afraid. You see, you change to human, I'll kill you as a human. You stay as a wolf, I'll kill you as a wolf. I'm no longer bound by those ridiculous constrictive moral guides your mother has placed on us for far too long.*

You are bound to her. My voice sounds feeble, even to me. *You can't go against the Alpha.*

Yes, bound by her rule of not hurting any of the gammas. But you're not in the pack anymore, are you?

You think she'll be okay with you killing me?

The thing is, Narissa. You've inspired me. I'm not sure I want to be part of her pack anymore either. You can consider this my first act in asserting my new position. Once you're dealt with, a heartbroken alpha should be no problem to dispose of. You've seen how emotional she gets over stray little gammas like Alena. I can't wait to see how she crumbles when she hears what's happened to her precious little daughter. And don't try to deny it. I know. I have people on the inside.

For the first time since facing Daniel, my attention leaves him and turns to Art. His head is bowed, and his tail is between his legs.

How could you? I trusted you.

His head snaps up with an angry snarl.

Freya is on borrowed time, and my mother blindly follows her around. Her way of doing things, all this compassion and forgiveness, is not going to last. It can't. Like this, I get to keep my mother safe.

You think it's going to be better with him in charge?

As he turns his head away from me, I leap forward, clawing his ear.

Answer me!

He's caught by surprise and jumps into the air with a yelp.

You owe me an answer! You betrayed me! And you've betrayed Freya and Chrissie and for what?

I told you. This will keep my mother safe.

No, it won't. She can think for herself, and she'd never choose Daniel. If anything, you've put her in even more danger. This isn't about her. You think helping him to take over will profit you. With him in charge, you'll be noticed. You won't be brushed aside by younger wolves that are infinitely more capable than you. Like your sister.

I'd watch what you're saying.

Art's growl is loud, but it doesn't faze me. Not in the slightest.

You think he's going to keep his word? He's used you and you were so desperate that you'd believe anything.

You don't understand.

Do I not? Because I can see in your head, remember. I can feel all that self-doubt in there. And it's deserved. You're right. You've never fitted in here. And you never will. What do they do to trai-

CHAPTER 36

torous wolves, Art? I don't think you ever did tell me. Is it banishment? Or is it a little more gruesome than that?

I am going to kill you.

He launches himself at me, but before he can reach me, Daniel is between us.

Enough. I don't care for your petty squabbles.

He clearly says something else to Art, who retreats with a whimper, once again adopting a submissive posture.

As much as we have some of the finer details of my leadership to iron out, this will not concern you, Narissa

Daniel's lips curl upwards, exposing his teeth.

It is time to end your life.

37

I can't outrun him forever. I know that, but I need time to find a way out of this predicament. Think, Narissa. Think. You've been in bad situations before. This is no worse than the Blood Bank. Dozens of vampires would have been happy to see you dead there. The same when you broke out of the dungeon. You escaped that. You'll escape this too. You just need to figure it out, to come up with a plan.

But the pep talk is not the blindest bit of use because I know the truth. Surviving those situations had nothing to do with my skills at all. Other people got me out of those holes I'd dug myself into. Rey and Calin. Even human-against-human—when Joe caught up with me—Calin was the one who saved me. No matter how much I think of myself as an independent woman, all the evidence is to the contrary.

So, with that in mind, I'm blindly running. Running like my damned life depends on it, which it does. The head start I got was minimal, but by some bloody miracle, I'm still in front, although for how much longer I daren't think; my lungs are already starting to burn.

Give up, little wolfie.

His voice comes through in my head, but I block it out with such force he yelps. Great. That slowed him down a fraction, but he won't risk that again and, at this precise moment, I've got nothing up my furry sleeves.

I'm less powerful and less fit than he is, but I'm also a whole chunk smaller and lighter. That's got to be worth something.

The morning light grows brighter as it filters through the leaves, dappling the forest floor. I think about those wildlife documentaries that Rey, Oliver and I used to watch together. We'd often end up viewing them by default, when we couldn't agree on a film, but the fact was, we all loved them. That surge of adrenaline, seeing a wild animal chase down its prey, then that sudden feeling of relief, when the innocent deer or wildebeest somehow escapes the jaws of doom. The adrenaline isn't so satisfying when it's my life on the line. Visions of gazelles on the Serengeti plains sweep through my mind. The way they would dart and dash in every direction, trying to throw the lions off their tracks.

That's it. The idea's a weak one, but it's better than nothing. Lighter animals can turn faster. That's how they get away. Never by running in straight lines, but by confusing their predators. By making them double back on themselves and slowing them down. Maybe it won't work, but right now, anything is worth a try.

Daniel is closing in as we approach one of the streams. I can feel the heat of his breath and hear the snapping of his jaws as he tries to get a hold of me. This is it, I think, as the stream comes into sight. It's a long jump, one he'll need to make too. I just need to get my timing right.

It's a move unlike any I've tried before. My front paws touch down on the far side of the stream. As my hind paws land right beside them, I twist my body back and over itself and then push off again with my back legs and fly straight over Daniel. His eyes widen in surprise as his head tilts up towards me. His jaws snap at my hindquarters, but he misses by a hair's breadth. Literally.

It's given me a greater lead over him, but it doesn't take him long to start eroding that again. I manage to keep evading him, using my smaller size and lightness to my advantage. Twisting and turning, I corkscrew my body away from his teeth, time and time again. But it's getting harder with every manoeuvre. My muscles aren't used to this. My legs, my chest, all along my back, aches. And I'm slowing down. I know I am. I might have agility, but there's not enough stamina to match it. Art was right about my physical fitness, if nothing else. I know I've got to make a choice. Blocking him from my head was the only way to make sure he couldn't anticipate my moves, but it's taking up energy that my body needs. In one last-ditch gamble, I let my barrier down.

His anger is the first thing that hits me. Pure, unadulterated fury.

CHAPTER 37

You little bitch! I was going to make it easy for you. Not now. Not a chance. You are going to suffer!

I want to make some sarcastic riposte, but I just don't have the strength. All I can do is keep twisting and turning, while trying not to think about what I'm going to do next. There's a thin branch over to my left. I wager it's strong enough to take my weight but not his. As I dart towards it, Daniel changes direction and blocks my route.

Shit

Don't worry, this will be over soon.

He's right. I can't run any more. I try to dodge him, but he blocks me once and then twice. We're in a small clearing and there's nowhere left for me to go. We slowly circle, our eyes locked on each other. I don't need to hear what he's saying to know what he wants. Me. Dead.

I'm going to enjoy this. His voice is in my head. *Perhaps you will, too. I've heard that the return to Eve is supposed to be incredibly exhilarating, once you let yourself go. What do you think, little wolfie? Are you ready to do that?*

Over my dead body.

Exactly.

I feel I should be able to muster one last defiant stand. Do something other than roll over and succumb to the inevitable, but when he pounces, that's it. The full weight of his body lands squarely on my shoulders, causing my legs to buckle. I topple sideways and my nose slams into the dirt. I can feel blood pooling around my face. And the pain! It's everywhere and it's consuming me.

I claw blindly, trying to get him to loosen his grip, to get some modicum of respite from the agony. Once or twice, I graze his fur and flesh, but mostly my claws connect with nothing but air. And the pain is getting even worse.

I can taste blood in my mouth. We're meant to heal faster as wolves, aren't we? I suppose there's only so much healing even wolf power can achieve, particularly when there's a three-hundred-pound wannabe alpha pressing down on your rib cage.

If only I'd had longer, to learn more about who I am and about Freya and my father.

I close my eyes, not knowing if I will ever open them again.

I wish I could say goodbye to Oliver. To apologise for everything, especially all the lying. I know it wouldn't be enough to mend our friendship, but I'd like to tell him how much he meant to me.

That's so sweet. Thinking of your boyfriend. I'll be sure to pass on your message.

So, this is how it ends. I can barely breathe now, and my vision is fading to black.

Get the fuck away from my daughter!

38

The snarling is so vicious, so intense, that the hairs along my back bristle. And I'm not the only one who's shocked. Daniel shifts off my chest.

I gasp for air. I have no strength left to block anything out, and whether I'm pack or not, I'm feeling the pure rage flowing from Freya.

What great timing, Daniel sneers as he steps off me entirely. *I assumed you'd have to take my word for how this scene went down, but now you can see it first-hand. The only question is, which one of you do I end first?*

Step away from Narissa.

Even in my head her enunciation is so clear it's like she's spitting the words at him.

I won't ask again, Beta.

Beta? You're not that naïve, Freya. This is a play for your crown, I'm afraid. One I'm very much planning on winning.

You'll have to fight me first

Oh, I plan on it, old wolf. I plan on fighting you to the end.

Really? So that's why you're stalling? Trying to catch your breath?

I'm not—

He doesn't get the chance to finish. At the periphery of my vision, I see my mother leap into the air. She passes clear over me, barrelling into Daniel and sending him sprawling. But, in less than a heartbeat, he's recovered and is on his feet again, snapping back at her.

Your day is over, Freya.

No, it's not.

Give it up. Relinquish your position to me immediately and I might just let you live and that bastard child of yours, too. I could use a plaything. Or, better still, perhaps I'll take her as my mate. The bloodline would be strong with that one.

This time, my mother lashes out with a paw, hitting him straight across the jaw. It's a knock that would have sent me flying, but he doesn't even flinch.

Is that all you've got? I would have tried this months ago, if I'd known how frail you've become.

This is your last chance, Daniel. Back down now. Submit, or I'll—

Or you'll what? Tell me off? Call me a bad wolf? This pack deserves a true leader. Someone who isn't afraid to make the tough decisions. To act in accordance with the old traditions.

Is that right?

In your heart, you know it's true.

Perhaps you're right. Perhaps I do.

I'm having a hard time seeing what's going on. As I attempt to roll over, a loud yelp escapes me, and I fall back. He's crushed some of my ribs, and I think one of my legs is broken, too.

Just stay down, Narissa, my mother's voice hisses in my head. *This will be over with soon.*

I fear she's right. Maybe it would have been better if she had just let him finish me and try to survive this herself. Apparently, I'm not the only one who thinks this.

Stop playing these games with me, Freya. You know this only ends one way.

Is that so?

I manage to stagger to my feet. I was right—my front leg is clearly broken. Adjusting my weight onto the other three, I shuffle through into the undergrowth and huddle down by a fallen tree trunk, from where I can see it all, including another wolf, standing off to one side, also watching.

Chrissie! I yell through my mind to her. *Help her. You must help her.*

The amber wolf stares at me with her green eyes.

I can't interfere. This is down to your mother.

He's too strong.

We have to let this play out.

But it was a trap. Art did this. He set us up to save you. You must help her.

A surge of emotion flashes through her.

No. He couldn't.

Please, Chrisse. He wants to kill her.

There's nothing I can do. This is how it works. Have faith in her.

Please, please help!

I can feel her pain and torment, but her resolve is fixed. She's not going to do anything, and I can't. I'm the one who got Freya into this situation and there's nothing I can do with my leg and ribs broken. Images of Rey swarmed by vampires fill my mind. Of Oliver, too, as he confronted Styx because of a trap I stupidly walked straight into. And now I've done it again.

The two wolves are fighting now, tumbling over one another, twisting back and forth. It's impossible to tell who's winning. It's a blur of claws, teeth and fur. Freya's white against Daniel's black, like a savage yin and yang. Blood is flying everywhere. But which one is it coming from? I can't tell. Now turning in circles, they snap at each other, looking for an opening.

This has gone on long enough, Alpha. Time to end it.

I think you're right.

They spring simultaneously and lock jaws on one another, Freya on his hind leg, but Daniel near her throat, and it looks like he's drawing blood. With a gut-wrenching tug, Freya yanks herself out of his grip and rolls onto her back.

It looks like she's about to submit. Daniel thinks so, too. I can tell by the way he pauses, as if to enjoy the moment. But this is all she needs. As he moves to stand over her, she jerks upwards, and her teeth clamp onto his throat. He tries to shake her off, but it does no good. If anything, it only makes matters worse. The more he struggles, the deeper and deeper her teeth sink and the more his flesh rips.

So, you don't think I have the strength to lead?

CHAPTER 38

He whimpers.

You have no idea what true power is. It isn't throwing your weight about, you fool. I have watched every one of your fights since you turned. I know each of your moves and all your strengths and weaknesses.

His legs buckle as he struggles to breathe, and Freya rolls him over so that she has him pinned to the ground. The fur at his neck is glistening red.

You don't think I can make the tough decisions? Well, how about this? You will never challenge me or anyone else ever again.

She releases her grip on his throat and slashes a paw at his face, digging her claws into the soft tissue of an eye. His howling startles the birds from the trees. As she steps away, I see blood pouring from the empty socket.

And now to deal with you, she says.

39

It's not every day you see your mother gouge out someone's eye. And it's not over yet.

With Daniel now lying there a whimpering wreck, her fury has barely lessened by a fraction. She has others to deal with. Starting with me. I went against her. I guess I didn't realise quite what that would mean, until now.

Chrissie. Her voice comes through clearly. *I take it you can handle Art.*

I will tear him limb from limb.

I leave the decision up to you. Whatever you think is a suitable punishment. But remember, he knows what his life will be from now on.

He and I both. I do not have the words to say how sorry I am. Deal with it swiftly.

Her attention comes back to me.

Narissa. The village! Now!

When it was just my dad and me, I never really got into any trouble. We were a team. We were all we had, and I made it my mission never to let him down, and I think I managed that pretty well. But to say my mother is disappointed in me is a massive understatement.

She doesn't address another word to me on the entire journey back home. And it's not because I'm blocking her. I'm not. I am wide open. I want her to feel my guilt at how much I've screwed up and realise I am in the wrong. She's the one blocking me and that's a wall I cannot get through.

When we reach the boundary of the forest and return to human, I pick up some clothes from the well and struggle to put them on. I was right. My left arm is broken. But I don't ask for help. The time spent as a wolf has helped it recover, but it's still a long way off healed, and purple and black bruises are blooming beneath the skin. I try not to wince at the pain as I finally manoeuvre a shift dress over my head.

My mother looks in an even worse state than me, although she barely flinches as she selects a shirt and slips her arms into the sleeves.

"I'm sorry," I call, running to catch up with her the best I can, as she marches off towards the village. "I just thought …"

"I told you not to leave the cabin."

"I know, but Art had been helping me. I didn't think there was any reason not to trust him."

"You're right. You had no reason not to trust him. But he is not the problem here. The relationship you had with Art is not what I am judging. It's how little you obviously trust me."

"That's not true," I say, but my voice is a whimper. A child's protest.

Finally, Freya stops and turns to face me. "Do you believe I would have kept you cooped up in the cabin if I thought it was safe for you to be out running in the forest? Do you really think that's how I wanted you to spend your last days here with me?"

"I don't know. I … I just wasn't thinking." As I stumble over my apology, I latch onto something. "My last days here? What do you mean? What are you going to do with me?"

With a long sigh, her expression softens from anger to resignation.

"I can't keep you safe here, Narissa. I was worried from the moment you arrived, but when you cast yourself away from us, I finally had to face facts: if you're not truly with us, then you'll always be outside us, and I will always be forced to choose between you and everyone else. You have seen how much danger you can get yourself into without the rules to protect you."

"But Daniel won't hurt me again. Not after what you did to him."

The memory of his missing eyeball returns momentarily, and I quickly force it away.

"There will always be Daniels," she says, with the first hint of sympathy in her voice. "Not to mention a whole heap of other threats neither of us has even thought of. Right now, Narissa, with members of my pack going missing and turning up dead, I can't even keep them safe. I don't know how long it will be until whatever it is ends up right on our doorstep. And when that happens, how do you expect me to choose? You or the pack. That's what it will come down to. I had to make that decision once before, Narissa. I don't think I could survive it a second time."

When she lifts her eyes to meet mine, they're full of tears and I realise mine are too. Great drops are spilling down my cheeks.

"What will happen to me?" I ask, fearfully. "Where can I go?"

With a sniff, Freya wipes the back of her hand across her face.

"I have spoken to Juliette, the Alpha of South Pack. She has agreed that you can stay there."

Another pack. Another set of rules and this time amongst complete strangers.

"I have to be part of her pack?"

"You don't have to. It's up to you. But I would advise you to accept the offer. You will be safer there."

"Why? If it's not safe for me to be here as a lone wolf, why would it be safer there?"

I know I've brought this on myself, but at the same time it feels like my heart is being torn from my chest. Like she's deserting me all over again.

"Her pack and her territory are larger. She has several lone wolves there. They are independent, but they also help each other when necessary. And, although it pains me to admit it, they are stronger than we are and not just in numbers. Daniel was right about one thing. My way of peace has benefits, but we are not like we used to be. We have been complacent about our safety for too long, while Juliette's pack has grown even more fearsome. If Calin is right and a vampire is behind the killing of Alena and the kidnapping of the others, then I fear a war is on the horizon. You will be better trained to deal with it there."

As she finishes speaking, there's a lump in my throat and my eyes begin to brim with tears again.

"When?" I choke out. "When am I going?"

"She will arrive the day after tomorrow to collect you."

I nod.

"Narissa, this doesn't have to be for ever. It may seem that way now. But maybe, in time, you will think about coming back."

I sniff and nod again, and she attempts to look less sad but fails.

"Would it make you feel a little better if I tell you I have arranged for a chaperone to go with you?"

"A chaperone?"

This time, she does manage a little smile as she tips her head towards the village and a figure who's standing on the edge of the field, staring at us. The early morning sun is warm, yet the person is covered from head to foot in black.

"Calin!"

And before I can stop myself, I find myself running to him.

40

Polidori

"Come in and close the door behind you," I say.

The heavy, velvet curtains are closed and will stay that way until the sun has moved around behind the building. There is no point in suffering unnecessary discomfort. Over the decades, I have learned what I can happily tolerate and how much I can endure if I must. I have even trained myself to withstand exposure to full sunlight for a short while. But that took years, rather like an athlete training their muscles or a linguist learning fluency in a new tongue.

"Please, sit down."

I remain seated as the human takes his place in the antique wingback chair opposite me. His pulse is fast, his breathing shallow. He's almost wheezing. The apparently confident way he'd knocked had been nothing more than bravado. He is terrified. He always is in these meetings although, today, I could smell it even as he opened the door.

"Is there something I can do for you?" he asks.

"There is. The wolf girl. She escaped. I want her dealt with."

"I … I understand, but I'm not sure how I can assist you with this. My relationship with the wolves is … tenuous at best."

"Don't worry about that. What I want to know is whether or not you are willing to do whatever is necessary."

"Such as?"

"Only time can tell."

His lips twist, eyes shifting away from me. I have known many in his position during my time with the Council. He's not the weakest, but he's a long way from the strongest. But that's good. I can use it to my advantage.

"You know we have our rules," he says, "specific ones, when it comes to interfering in this type of thing."

Another attempted display of strength, but I play along.

"I do. And I respect that. If this situation were in any way normal, I wouldn't even consider asking, but please, take a look at this …"

Opening a desk drawer, I pull out a piece of cream paper. The text on it is typed, and it bears my signature at the bottom.

CHAPTER 40

"What is it?" he asks, accepting the document.

"Consider it a gesture of goodwill. Or, if you rather, a little incentive to help you come round to my way of thinking. I am, as you know, a man of my word, but I know that you modern men like your contracts. Please, be my guest. Read through it. It's all fairly standard."

Sitting back in my chair, my lips twitch as I hear his pulse quicken. This time, it's with excitement, not fear. Adrenaline is flooding his system; I can almost taste it.

"I didn't think you did this. I didn't know this was an option."

"Ordinarily, it's not. But, given all the cooperation you've extended to us over the years, I think I could persuade the Council to make an exception in this case."

The cogs and wheels are obviously turning as he weighs up the pros and cons. I've seen this so many times. They genuinely believe they have a choice. But the answer is the same every time. Still, I can see he needs a little prompting.

"You asked me many years ago. Do you remember? Long before you were in the position you hold now. And I said we would have to see what the future brought. Well, the future has arrived. Are you no longer interested in this?"

"I ... I just never imagined it would ever happen."

"It won't, not immediately. I will need your help resolving a few *issues* first. But then, if you decide this is what you want ..."

His eyes go from the paper to me and back again. He

runs a finger down it, as if double-checking what's written there.

"Yes," he says, quietly, then more forcefully: "Yes, this is exactly what I want."

"Fantastic. So can I assume I'll have your full cooperation and assistance in whatever is to come?"

"Whatever you need. I'll do it."

41

Narissa

A girl sprinting across a field towards a dark, handsome man standing with his arms open, sounds like something from a film adaptation of a Jane Austen novel. All you need is the slo-mo effect to complete the scene. That is, until it's revealed that the girl is a broken werewolf, and the man is a vampire.

If the last week has taught me anything, it's that I'm far more of a cliché than I ever thought possible. I used to watch horror movies with Rey and Oliver—Rey's choice, not ours—and always balked at those ridiculous girls in high heels who would run in the wrong direction in any dangerous situation or hurry to a car they didn't have the keys to. And if they ever started walking backwards, well you knew it was all over. Yet running towards Calin feels exactly right and completely normal.

"An eventful couple of days, I take it," he says, smiling as he gently touches one of the many bruises on my face, before his eyes widen in horror as he sees my mother approaching us, equally battered. "Please don't tell me you challenged her."

"Hell, no. Thank God." I dip my head. "So, you haven't heard about what happened with Daniel?"

"No." He shakes his head. "Freya just said you weren't safe here anymore and asked me if I'd go with you to the South Pack. What happened?"

I go to take a deep breath to start explaining, but it sends a searing pain shooting across my chest.

"How about I tell you over a drink? Please, tell me you brought alcohol."

It's a stark contrast to the last time we were in here together, struggling to keep our clothes on. Instead, we sit together at the small table. He had brought whisky. I don't know if it's his expensive one or not, but I really don't care. Just as I don't care that it's barely ten in the morning and I'm already on the hard stuff. The liquid burns my throat in a very satisfying way, and when my glass is empty, I pick up the bottle and help myself to another.

"I feel like such an idiot," I tell him. "I was just so

fixated on getting her out of my head. On not letting her control me. I didn't stop to think that there might be consequences. And Art ... how the hell did I not see through his lies?"

"There was nothing to see through. He thought he was doing the right thing. And I'm sure he deeply regrets his actions."

It's hard not to think about what my mother did to Daniel and wonder what sort of punishment Chrissie will mete out on Art. He's her son, but does that mean she'll go easy on him or be harsher with her punishment? I suspect I already know the answer to that.

"Tell me about London," I say, trying to shut out the image of Art with only one eye, or worse. "Did you talk to Polidori? Did he say anything about me? Did you tell him I was innocent?"

The dip of his chin tells me this isn't going to be good news.

"He was not in a receptive mood. I couldn't even broach the subject."

"Couldn't or wouldn't?" I snap, then hurriedly shake my head apologetically. "I'm sorry. I just need some good news for once. The sooner he stops wanting me dead, the sooner I can leave."

"I know, but I think you need to prepare yourself for the long haul. He's not in a good place right now. In fact, he's not in a place I've ever seen him before. He's convinced the wolves are plotting against us. Witches too. He's become paranoid that they want to overthrow us."

"What will he do?"

"I don't know. He's normally so level-headed."

Great. It's tough enough knowing my actions resulted in the death of one of my friends, but if Calin's right and Polidori really is out for vengeance, then I could end up having a lot more blood on my hands. It's not difficult to work out where he got the idea about witches from, either. Another minus point for me. I cup my head in my hands.

"Hey," Calin says, reaching across to me. "It's okay. This will be all right. It will. For you and the wolves. You just need to have a little patience."

"I know." I try to sound convincing. But that's the thing with having a heart-to-heart with a vampire who can hear your heartbeat. He knows full well I'm lying. I knock back the second whisky

"Is there anything I can do?" he asks, pouring me another before I can refuse. "What do you want from me?"

What *do* I want from him? A few nights ago, I would have had a very clear idea, but the truth is, I'm exhausted. I may have only been on the run for a week, but it feels like years and I'm not sure how long I can keep it up. There's a chance this negativity is partly due to pain and lack of sleep. It would be so lovely to curl up in bed with someone's arms wrapped reassuringly around me. So that's what I tell him.

"Whatever you need," he responds.

42

I sleep for hours. By the time I wake, the sun has already moved well past its zenith and the sky is a deep azure blue. Every muscle has seized, and my left arm is throbbing all the way from the wrist to the shoulder. Maybe if I sleep a little longer it will heal some more. Maybe I should just hibernate until everything's dealt with.

"You're awake," Calin says, despite the fact that I've not moved. "How do you feel? Better?"

Grimacing at the pain, I twist around to face him, only to find he's closer than I thought. Our noses are practically touching. The temptation to plant my lips on his is almost irresistible. That would be a good distraction, another way to keep my mind occupied until Juliette turns up. But it doesn't feel right this time, and instead, I shuffle back a fraction.

"I don't know," I say, honestly. "I heal faster when I'm a wolf. Maybe I need to head to the forest for a couple of hours. Although I don't know if I'm allowed to do that now. I should probably check with Freya."

"Well, who would have imagined? All it took was yet another near-death experience and you've actually started listening to people."

It's tempting to make a snide remark, but it turns out he's right, and I find myself smiling.

"So, is there anything you need to do before Juliette arrives? Anyone you want to say goodbye to?"

"Actually, there is."

It's ridiculous how nervous I feel. My heart is pounding, and I have considered turning and walking away a dozen times, but the fact is, I need to know. I need to see Lou, to see Chrissie and apologise, because whatever trouble Art got into, I know on some level it's got to be my fault. I never used to be one of those people who disaster followed around, but lately it's felt like there's a neon sign flashing directly above my head, directing chaos straight to me.

For over a minute, I stare at their front door. More than once, I lift my hand to knock, and then don't. Maybe it would be better to just go. There's a good chance I'm the last person they want to see. Shaking my head, I drop my hand again and start to turn away, when the door swings open.

"Naz."

CHAPTER 42

Lou's eyes are red-rimmed, and her skin is pale, where it's not blotchy. The sight of her makes my stomach squirm with guilt.

"I ... I'm sorry," I stutter, stepping back. "I shouldn't have c—"

She jumps through the doorway, wraps her arms around me and nearly suffocates me in a painful hug.

"Don't you dare. Don't you dare apologise. *I* am the one who's sorry. I can't believe it. I can't. I mean, I don't want to. I thought he was better than that. He's such a dick. I don't even have the words to tell you how sorry I am. Please, please come in."

This outpouring has a surprisingly comforting effect, and I follow her into the house.

Despite it being afternoon, the curtains are closed, and dirty dishes are piled in the sink.

"Do you want a coffee?" she asks, as I take a seat on the sofa. "I probably shouldn't have another one. There's no way I'll sleep tonight. I think I'll have to go for a run. Maybe we could go together, if you'd like that? Before Juliette arrives?"

"You've heard then?" I say, before responding about the drink. "A coffee would be great."

"Mum told me bits and pieces. Actually, she probably told me everything. I think she needed to unburden. It's not fair. You shouldn't have to go anywhere. We should be able to keep you safe here. Although Juliette's wolves are notoriously ferocious. You know they get transformed as soon as they're old enough to talk."

"You said."

A small pause follows. "Maybe you'll get along all right there. You are a pretty kick-arse wolf yourself."

I manage a small smile, but it only lasts for a moment. As nice as this conversation is, it's not the reason I came.

"Lou, about Art—"

"Don't," she says, raising a hand to stop me. "Don't even mention his name."

"Please, I just want to know what happened to him. I need to know if he's okay."

"You should want to know he's dead. That used to be the penalty for defying the Alpha. I wish it still was."

"You can't mean that. He's your brother."

"And so are half the people in the pack."

"But not in the same way."

"Maybe not, but …" She pauses to put water in the coffee machine. "I've known everyone here since the day I was born. Or they were. We look after one another. That's the way it has always been since Eve. The only way we survive is by working together."

"But you said trying to overthrow the Alpha is something that happens. Just part of pack life."

"Yes, when the Alpha is weak or old or making bad decisions. None of those apply to Freya. Daniel wanted control because he wanted the power. That's it, pure and simple. And, in my view, wolves are like politicians: anyone who wants it that badly shouldn't be allowed to have it. But at least we all knew where we stood with him. What Art did was worse. And I brought him to meet you. He fooled me. I should have known better."

While all of this is strangely reassuring to hear, it still hasn't answered my question.

"So, what has happened to him? Where is he now?"

Lou pulls out the mug from the coffee machine and hands it to me, before drawing in a long breath and letting it slowly out again.

"Mum dealt out the same punishment to him as Freya did to Daniel."

"His eye?" Oh God, I feel sick. "Will it heal? Will it return to normal?" I ask. Wolf healing would seem kind of pointless if it didn't work on important things like that, but Lou's shaking her head.

"No. We can heal things fast that need repairing, like that," she says, gesturing to my arm. "A couple of good runs and you'll be fine again. But we can't regrow things."

Shit, this is even worse than I imagined.

"That's barbaric."

"Freya used to think so, but not anymore, apparently. And I get it. With the way things are, those two can't be allowed a voice anymore. This has stripped them of that."

"They are still in the pack?"

"She wouldn't kick them out. Besides, anyone in their right mind wouldn't let them out of their sight, but they've no status now. They're lower than the gammas."

"I bet Daniel loves that."

"Well, he's only got himself to blame. He knew the risk he was taking."

The realisation that Art is still part of the pack and

therefore still a member of this family, makes me worry he could return here at any moment. That, combined with the door swinging open, causes me to jump up with such speed that I spill hot coffee all over myself.

"Narissa."

"Freya." I put my mug down on the table, wiping at the spill on my T-shirt. "I'm sorry. I know I didn't ask if it was okay to go out. I wanted to come and see Lou. To say goodbye."

"It's fine. I was looking for you, to suggest you go for a run. Well, a walk perhaps. Get some healing in. You'll want to have your injuries sorted by the time Juliette arrives in the morning."

I don't know if she means on my own or with her, but either way it doesn't matter. The answer is the same.

"That would be great," I say.

43

"I was worried about you," Calin says, when I return to the cabin only a short while before sunset.

I would have stayed out longer, only it started raining. The light drizzle was refreshing at first, and the others didn't seem to mind too much. But wet fur is not something I'm ready to embrace just yet. The walk was exactly what I needed. Within an hour, the pain in my arm and the rest of my body had lessened to the point where I could run. Not fast and not for long, but the healing seems exponential and I'm already feeling so much better.

"If you were really worried about me, you would have come looking for me."

"You're right. I knew you'd be okay. How were things with Freya? Did you two talk?"

"Not a lot, but that's fine. There'll be time. I did say that once I'm settled with Juliette, I'll come back and visit. Lone wolf status has its advantages."

He's sitting on the bed, a book on his lap, looking every bit the devilishly handsome vampire, which I try to ignore.

"How are you feeling about the Juliette situation?"

"What choice do I have? Where else is there for me to go?"

"If you don't feel safe—"

"They'll protect me. Freya's certain they will. Right now, that's enough. To be honest, I just want a few days, a couple of weeks even, to sleep and recover and not think about anything. I'm exhausted, Calin."

"I'm not surprised." His eyes wander over to the table, to the map my mother brought me. "I've been meaning to ask you. What's that? Is it the land around here?"

I bring it over and sit on the edge of the bed next to him.

"It belonged to Freya and my dad. They marked all the places they went to on it and where they agreed he'd meet her, to rescue her."

"So, you two have been talking."

"Just a little."

I trace a finger over the lines of latitude and longitude. They are barely visible now and some have disappeared altogether in the folds. Only now do I have the slightest inkling of how difficult it must have been for her. One week is all I've had here and not even as a full member of the pack. The closest I've got to meeting them all is when I thought they were going to ambush us when we first arrived. And I've only made one friend. Yet

I already feel a sense of grief at what I'm leaving behind, at the loss of a family I could have known. How much must she have loved my father to leave with him like that? How is it possible to love someone that strongly so quickly? I don't know. All I do know is that Freya leaving here and then leaving us, wasn't nearly as black and white as I'd always imagined.

Calin's gaze is lost on the map, his fingers now moving between the marks I showed him. After a minute, I gently pull it out of his grasp and fold it back up. Talking to him has taken my mind off things for a little while, but if this is the last night we're going to be together, possibly for ever, then looking at maps and grieving over my parents is not how I want it to be.

"What do you think about getting an early night?" I suggest, standing up so that I can straddle him and slowly lowering myself onto his lap. For a split second, I think I might have got it wrong. That the time he spent away from me will have been enough to convince him that messing around like this is a bad idea. But a groan leaves his lips before I'm even seated. As I press my chest against his and kiss him, he responds without hesitation. This is definitely a much better way to spend the evening.

Maybe I should have got some sleep. Morning has come around fast, and today's the day I meet the Alpha of a different wolf pack. One who holds my fate in her hands. But sleeping would have only let the nightmares in, and I didn't want to dream. I wanted to live. Every time we're together it is better than the last, each minute an opportunity for us to explore each other's bodies further.

As I lie there, nestling in his embrace, he runs a finger up and down the length of my arm.

"Are you thinking about today?" he asks. "About Juliette?"

"I guess," I say. "Yes, a bit."

It's not entirely true; there's another thought that's worked its way into my mind and not for the first time. Whenever he stopped distracting me with his kisses, it found another route in. Why, when I thought Daniel was about to kill me, was it Oliver I wanted to see for one last time? I know I needed to apologise to him, and for so long he's been the closest thing I had to family. But he's not family or even a boyfriend. I didn't think about Freya other than how disappointed in me she'd be and her possible grief. I did think of Calin, but it was Oliver I wanted at the end. Does that have some particular significance? He's been like a brother to me. Maybe that was it. It's got to be.

"We should get dressed," Calin says, stirring me from my thoughts. "Juliette's arriving soon. I don't somehow think finding her newest recruit in the arms of vampire would put you on the right footing."

"I'm a lone wolf, remember?" I say, twisting to face him.

"Of course. I apologise. You think she'll be okay with that?"

"No, probably not. We should get a shower."

"Together?"

"Really, act your age. You are a hundred years old."

"A hundred and twenty-five, to be precise, and last night you said experience was a good thing."

I move to swipe the pillow from underneath him, but he grabs my hand. His eyes lock on mine, and the playfulness evaporates. A calm seriousness returns.

"I'm not going to give up, Narissa. Somehow, I will make Polidori see he's got the wrong idea about the wolves. You just have to stay out of trouble until I manage it, okay?"

"Me? Trouble?"

His glower deepens. "I mean it."

"I know. Come on, we need to get up or we'll be late."

"Maybe we could manage another hour?"

"I said we'd have breakfast at Freya's first."

"You did what?"

"THESE PANCAKES ARE GOOD," I say, as we sit at the table in my mother's cabin. Calin has declined the offer of both food and whisky and is politely sipping a glass of orange juice. A vampire drinking orange juice. I love it.

"I'll be honest. Chrissie made them. I've just been keeping them warm in the oven until you got here."

"Well, you've kept them warm very nicely."

"Thank you."

The conversation is stilted. But it's nowhere near as bad as the last time we were here, when we struggled to even look at each other. But now that's all we're doing for the most part, looking. There are a thousand things we should say but can't quite manage. I'm trying to convince myself everything will be all right. Like I said to Calin, this isn't the end. I've got my mother back. It'll take time, but we can work on and repair what's broken. I know we can.

As we finish eating, Calin is the first to stand.

"Thank you, Calin, for looking after my daughter. We should probably say our goodbyes now. Juliette will be here soon. I thought she'd have already arrived already, actually. The heavy rain on the tracks last night has probably slowed her down."

"I'll go and check," he says. "I'm sure they won't be long."

"He's a good one," Freya says to me. "If only he had a pulse and was a fraction younger, I'd encourage you to keep seeing him," she jokes.

"A pulse can be overrated," Calin quips back, as he leans in and kisses her on both cheeks.

It's a surreal moment. Is this what it would have been like had she stayed with me and Dad? Would I be bringing boys for breakfast and laughing with her over her bad cooking?

CHAPTER 43

"I'll meet you back at the cabin?" he says to me, pulling his hat down to cover his face.

I nod. "I won't be long."

The moment he's gone, the awkwardness returns.

"Thank you—"

"I'm sorry—"

We say together, and the embarrassed smiles are mirror images.

"You go first," Freya says.

"I was just going to thank you and apologise that I didn't make this last week easy."

"I didn't make the last twenty years easy on you, Narissa. It is my greatest regret. I hope you know that."

"I do."

"And having you here, even for this short time. It's … It's like I was given a second chance. And I'm so sorry I didn't get that right, either."

"That was not all you."

"No, a lot of it is on you, but you are my daughter. I should have been prepared for such an impressive amount of stubbornness."

She pauses, and we fall silent again, but this time I catch it before it settles.

"We'll see each other again soon, I'm sure."

"We will. We have a lot of catching up to do."

And, just like that, I want to hug her. I want to absorb her scent and fix it in my mind before we part. Commit to memory the feel of her embrace. I step towards her, arms out, when Calin bursts through the door.

"We have a problem. A serious problem."

44

"What's the matter?" Freya asks.

"I've just been up the approach road. When did you last speak to Juliette? What does she know?"

"She knows the truth. That Narissa needs a safe place. That's there's trouble brewing with the vampires. Why?"

"Because there are two cars approaching and both are full of vampires. I could make out the engine of a third car, but the scent suggests a human and it appears to be going in a different direction."

"And Juliette?"

"She is in one of the cars," Calins says.

"That's impossible. Juliette would never mix with vampires like that."

"She's with them, Freya. At least half a dozen. Maybe more."

"They've taken her hostage, then. That's the only

possible explanation." Freya grabs my hands. "You must run!"

"What? No! I won't leave you with vampires coming here."

"Your mother is right. You're a liability, Narissa. She can tell them you've gone, that you ran off in the night. You have to do what she says."

"And then what? Just hide in the forest? They'd be able to track me. Hunt me down."

"We can mask your scent. I'll send the other wolves out to run with you," Freya says.

"I'm not doing this."

"You don't have a choice. This is the only way to make sure you're safe."

"I need a moment to think," I protest, clutching my head.

"You don't have one," Calin says, calmly, before turning to Freya. "Narissa showed me a map last night. How big is the spot where Michael picked you up? What's the terrain like there?"

"It's a narrow road ending in a small clearing."

"How small is small?"

She shakes her head. "Maybe the size of a couple of tennis courts?"

"No overhangs. No trees blocking it?"

"No, I don't think so. Although I've not been there in a while. Nothing substantial would have grown since then, though."

Nodding briefly, Calin turns back to me. "That's

where you need to go, Narissa. Run to that clearing and wait."

"For what?"

"When it's safe, one of us will come for you. I promise. But you must leave now."

I turn back to my mother, shock holding back my tears.

"I ... I ..."

"I know," she says, wrapping her arms around me and pulling me close. "I know. We'll talk about it later. Right now, you need to run."

We head out of her door. My legs are wobbling. Even if it's not forever, I need another hug. But when I turn around, she's gone, and once again in her place stands the most magnificent wolf I have ever seen, dazzlingly white in the morning sun.

"I thought wolves weren't allowed in the village," I gasp.

Then her howl rends the air. Soon a hundred others rise up to join it and my very soul feels on fire.

"Run, Narissa!" Calin yells above the din. "Run!"

45

Freya

She's gone. I watch as she dashes across the field towards the well and then out of sight, and my heart wants to explode. I want to run with her. I want to stay by her side. But the vampires are coming, and I'm her main line of defence. Hers and Juliette's. I need to protect them both. I have to protect everyone.

The pack immediately responded to my cry. Over two dozen have gone with her. They will guide her to the spot Calin told her to go to and cover her scent as she travels. They will protect her. Now it's my turn.

I change back to human. The vampire, Calin, is still beside me.

"Do you have a plan for her? Can you keep her safe?" I ask.

"*We* will keep her safe. What do you need of me?"

"How many of them are there? Can you tell? Do you know them?"

"Not from here. Freya, I don't think I need to tell you this, but if it gets back that I was with her, it will be harder for me to keep her safe in the long run, to clear her name for what she did to Styx."

"I understand. I put my pack above my daughter all those years ago, but when I see the marvellous young woman she's become, I don't regret it. Go to the Council and to Blackwatch. Fight for her. Clear her name. And find out who or what is killing us. That is what you can do for her and for me. For us all."

"I need somewhere out of sight to leave my car."

"There are plenty of barns. I'll get you the keys to one."

I go to move, but he catches my hand. Not hard, just a signal that he has more to say.

"Freya, if this turns into a fight."

"You can't choose sides. I know. But it won't come to that. Whatever these vampires are attempting, they've severely underestimated our numbers. Even a hundred of them wouldn't be a match for us. Hide your car, gather up your things, and do what you can to make sure my daughter is safe. You understand?"

"I do. And for your part, if nothing else, delay them."

I instinctively turn towards the rolling hills. There, weaving along the lane, are flashes of reflected light. At a guess I'd say there are two, maybe three cars. It's time to rally the troops.

CHAPTER 45

I DON'T REMEMBER the last time I checked my reflection in a mirror like this, combing back my hair to ensure no stray wisps cover my eyes. Appearance has never been important to me as a leader, but sometimes needs must. There's a reason they call it war paint. Daniel's words still echo. My inability to make the tough choices, to be brutal. But I would rip every vampire to shreds before I'd let them anywhere near my daughter. I've let her down enough. Not this time.

"What do you know?" Chrissie asks, as we walk towards the green and the only vehicular entrance.

"Only what the vampire told me. Juliette is not on her own. She has several escorts. Several *vampire* escorts."

"And you believe him?"

"You've seen how he looks at Narissa. He's risked his life for her. Besides, she trusts him, and that's enough for me."

"Are you're sure you don't want me to send out some scouts? It seems wrong, just waiting here for them to turn up. We should be on the front foot."

"Alena was a scout." That says it all. "They have Juliette. They have an alpha. Until we have a better grasp on what the situation is, I don't want anyone leaving the village."

Her disagreement is so strong, I can almost sense her biting her tongue. Some days, I value that about her. She's been my best friend almost my entire life. Her ability to question me is what keeps this partnership and pack working so well. But, right now, I don't want to be second-guessed. Thankfully, she knows that.

"What do you think this is? Do you think she's told them that Narissa is here?"

"I can't believe that. This is Juliette. However different her methods of leadership are, she's Alpha. Wolves come first. She told me she would take care of Narissa. She gave me her word. Whatever else I think of her, I know enough to be certain she wouldn't break it."

"I hope you're right," Chrissie replies.

Another minute passes. We stand in silence, staring out. In the distance, cars crawl closer down the hillside towards us.

"I think we are about to find out."

46

I have been scared many times in my life. Petrified, in fact. I recall being so terrified that my muscles seized up and my heart raced so fast, I thought it might burst. Yet here I still am, ready to fight another battle.

I was only fourteen years old at my ceremony, and I thought I knew it all and was ready for what was to come. I was excited about the future, and only a little nervous. But when the vampire's razor-sharp, venom-laced nail penetrated my skin and my bones snapped and reformed for the very first time, the pain of the transition set my whole body on fire. *Then* I was scared.

When I became a wolf, many new things frightened me. The things I had to do. The thing I was *made* to do. There is very little so terrifying in life as being entirely under someone else's absolute command, of not even being in control of your own mind. Having to blindly obey orders, regardless of what your conscience is telling you. That was why I left.

But nothing, in all my years of fighting and running, or claiming and maintaining my place as head of this pack, was even close to how scared I felt seven days ago, knowing that, after twenty years apart, I was going to see my daughter again. Realising that she would judge me for what I had done to her. Knowing that I deserved to be judged.

I've thought about her every day of her life. Wondered how she was coping, first without me and then her father. What her dreams were. Who she had grown up to become. Where her life would lead her. And, throughout all my daydreaming, somewhere in the back of my mind, I imagined what I would say to her, should she ever come to me. Deep down, I didn't think that would ever happen. I believed she was lost to me forever. Now I'm worrying that she could be again but permanently this time.

So, as I stand waiting at the entrance to our compound, I know I will protect my daughter no matter the cost.

Two vehicles are clearly in sight now, weaving their way slowly towards us, as they navigate the difficult terrain. They are close enough that the wolves standing behind me shudder at the scent, as they test the air.

There's only one road into our village. Thick forest, gorges and rivers block the approach from any other direction. There's no way by foot for anyone to go off track who doesn't know this area well, without them getting lost for days.

The vehicles are large, with bull bars across the front

bumpers and tinted windows, just like the car Calin came in, which is now hidden under a load of sacks in one of the barns. I am grateful that he was only here one night this time and didn't spread his scent too widely. When Narissa left, I burnt the clothes I was wearing this morning in a metal bin behind my house.

Beside me, Chrissy turns from wolf to human.

"Freya, I'm worried. The wind smells of death. The other wolves sense it, too."

"What else is a vampire, if not death? Could you detect Juliette?"

"I think so. There are traces of wolf, but they seem masked. They must have ambushed her, taken her hostage and somehow contained her."

Exactly. And, asking her to leave her pack to come and get Narissa, I had provided them with the perfect opportunity to do this, while she was on her own and vulnerable, just as Alena had been.

"We can get her out," I say, trying to convince myself as much as my Beta.

"By killing the vampires? Freya, that would bring a war to our doorstep."

"They have already done that. Besides, with no evidence, there can be no blame, and I don't plan on leaving any. Calin told me there was a man with them, too. Allowing for Juliette, there can't be more than ten vampires in those vehicles."

"I didn't pick up the scent of a human. Do you think he's a hostage too?"

"Possibly."

As the cars breach the final hill, I know we only have minutes left.

Summoning all the determination I possess; I turn and lift a hand. Immediately, hundreds of wolves turn into hundreds of humans. This was my mother's preferred way of addressing the whole pack, too.

"I am not here today to lie to you, pretend I know what is going to happen when those cars arrive. You know me better than that. Instead, I will tell you what I believe and hope my words ring true.

"After so many years of peace, we have had to face the shock of friends and family members going missing, even being killed. These are dark times, the likes of which most of you have never experienced. But we stand united, and we can overcome anything together. And let us not forget that our mother, Eve, was forged in pain, uncertainty and fear. That heritage runs through the veins of each and every one of us and will supply us with the courage and strength we may need today.

Worried glances are exchanged. Very few relish the idea of a fight, no matter how easily it might be won.

"We are not looking for trouble," I reassure them. "We are here as a family, protecting our own, not as a show of force. But neither will we be intimidated. Undivided, we are strong, and we stand here as one pack. *One pack!*"

"One pack!"
"One pack!"
"One pack!"

The hairs on my arms rise at the sound of their

voices echoing my words. Now they are turning to embrace one another. Is this just to offer encouragement? Or do they believe this could be farewell?

As I reflect on this, there's the sound of an approaching car and then the rumble as its wheels cross the cattle grid.

"Here we go," I whisper.

47

Juliette is a legend amongst legends. She is the oldest alpha to have ever lived and the longest serving. This alone would be impressive enough, but it is even more so when you consider what our lives entail. Alpha is not a role that is conducive to longevity. Before my mother's time, few were lucky to make it to fifty, many dying much younger, succumbing to the toll on both body and mind from constantly defending their position.

But Juliette has been the exception.

To say she rules with an iron fist would be doing her a disservice. Iron can be bent and moulded. It is malleable. Juliette is not.

The day she started her reign, everything changed. Only seventeen, yet her skills outstripped those of the most experienced wolf. Age should not matter, she decided, and there was therefore no need for anyone to wait until sixteen to receive the venom. Now, five- and six-year-olds, sometimes even younger children, are transformed as soon as they are deemed old enough to follow basic instructions. Wolves are allowed to roam her village day and night and if an accident happens because a newly turned wolf loses control in a public place, well, it teaches everyone to always be on their guard.

She normally keeps at least half a dozen betas, and it doesn't matter if they aren't the strongest in her pack. She chooses them for one thing only. Loyalty. There cannot be even a hint of dissension in the ranks. A combination of loyalty and fear is how she's reigned so long. It's not something I could do, but I admire her all the same. Besides, our different leadership skills don't matter right now. She's in the hands of vampires, and that's all that matters to me.

Chrissie stands at my side. My one and only Beta. I should have found a replacement for Daniel immediately, but I wanted to give it my full consideration first. His appointment had been a huge mistake, my faith in him totally misplaced. But hindsight is a wonderful thing. I'd thought it would satisfy his need for power. Look how that turned out.

"Should something happen to me …" I whisper to Chrissie.

"Don't."

"They trust you. They will honour your decisions."

"You know my thoughts on being an alpha. Nothing is going to happen to you. I will make sure of it."

"I'm glad to hear that."

Only one car door opens. I know in an instant that it's Juliette. Slowly, elegantly, she steps out and closes it behind her. She's approaching seventy, but stand us together, and you'd be hard pressed to say who's the younger. She's dressed entirely in black and is wearing a large, silver necklace. Her hair is pure white and close-cropped. She's never been much of a smiler, so I'm surprised to see a glimmer in her eyes as they meet mine, particularly on such a serious occasion.

"This is quite the welcoming party," she says.

"You understand."

"I do."

This is the disadvantage of being in human form. If we were wolves, there would be none of this. We would convey our exact thoughts instantly, without the need to pick our words carefully and try to work out any hidden meaning in what we hear. No ambiguity and nothing lost in translation.

For the longest moment, we stand there, eyes locked on one another. I can sense the tension behind me as the pack waits to see what will happen next. But I'm in no rush. The longer I can stall, the longer Narissa has to get away

"Are you okay," I ask.

"I will be."

I nod slowly, still trying to get a reading from her, but I can't. She is, and always has been, a closed book, but in a situation like this, I would have hoped she'd help me to pick up something, even if it's fear. Then again, what is there to be fearful of? She knows we can end this for her. And we will if that's what it takes.

"How did they find you? What do they want?" I ask.

She takes a deep breath and then slowly scans the pack, almost member by member. She has to be scared, but the way she's holding herself, as if she has everything under control, seems to say otherwise. I know she's arrogant, but this is just bizarre.

"Times are changing, Freya. You need to hand her over."

"What?"

"It's the only viable option, for all of us."

My fists clench. She notices. I force my anger back down and slowly release them.

"Juliette, whatever they've said to you. Whatever they've told you they'll do, we can protect you. You know we can."

"You can't even protect yourselves," she replies, with a snort of contempt.

"Look at our numbers. You think they'd stand a chance?"

"Numbers? You don't get it, do you? It doesn't count any more how big your army is. What matters are the weapons you've got on your side."

She looks back towards the cars, and another door swings open. Out steps a female vampire, dressed in jeans, a long-sleeved top, gloves on her hands and with a cap pulled down low over her head. She moves to the back of the vehicle, opens the boot, removes something and tosses it towards us.

"No," I gasp.

"No!" echoes from behind me. Two of my pack break ranks and I don't stop them. Lying in the dust, barely recognisable, is the body of Freddy, Alena's brother.

"I think the time for talking is over, don't you?" Juliette says.

And, for once, I am lost for words.

"Join us, Freya. There are great things planned. For all of us."

"With the vampires! What are you doing Juliette? What hold have they got on you?"

"Is that what you think? Why does one have to fail for others to succeed? A rising tide lifts all ships. And I'm tired of hiding in the shadows. Aren't you? Look at this place. You are a queen, Freya. You deserve a palace. Your name should be known throughout the world."

"I've never been one for the spotlight," I say, dryly.

She scoffs. "Ah, yes, and of course it all has to be about what *you* want. What about the rest of your pack? What about the new generation, Freya? You are stuck in ways that serve no purpose anymore. Give them the girl. Hand her over to the Council. Then you can have it whatever way you choose, join me and increase in power or stay here in your hovel and live on turnips and beetroot. Either way, it doesn't matter to me. But you know how this will end for you all if you don't co-operate."

Tension buzzes in the air around me as my pack waits to see what comes next.

"I would face every one of those monsters single-handedly before I'd surrender my child."

Juliette sighs.

"I'll lay my cards on the table now, Freya. You don't have to fight them. You have to fight me. I'm here to claim your pack."

48

Chrissie

As children, we squabbled daily. One minute we were best friends, the next we were tearing one another's hair out, swearing that we would never speak to each other again. I guess you could say we behaved like typical siblings would, and in many ways we were. But then, at our ceremony, everything changed.

I'm older than Freya, only by a year, but that day I felt it mattered. We were lined up in the hall, having listened to the usual passages from the Tale of Eve, waiting for the venom. It was by pure chance that I was standing next to her. Twelve of us were to be changed that year and she was the youngest, still so small and slight. Her eyes never once left the vampire who would administer the venom. The Alpha at the time—Freya's

CHAPTER 48

mother—accompanied him as he progressed from one end of the row. I can't remember who was the first to be turned. Some boy. His howl was so awful, I was gripped with terror. I was not the only one to be afraid. It's impossible to hear screams and witness agony like that and not be affected. I reached out and grabbed the nearest thing. Freya

She simply turned to me and calmly said, "This is what we were born for, Chrissie. You will survive it, and you will be great because of it." And at that moment, I knew she could lead me anywhere.

The day she disappeared, and we all thought she'd been killed, a part of me died, and I became harder. But I believe this gave me the strength to become who I am today. To become a beta. Strange as it may sound, thinking I'd lost her was the best thing that could have happened to me. Second only to her return.

As I stand here, watching the two alphas facing up to each other, I remember that ceremony and how I believed I would always follow her, even to war. That's about to be tested.

"This is ridiculous!" I step forwards, but Freya's arm blocks me from going any further.

"So, this is what it's all about, Juliette? You want my pack?" Freya's eyes bore into her.

"Yes, but first, I want the girl."

"You know that won't happen."

"Then you leave me no choice."

The frustration is killing me. My Alpha wants me to stay back. But Freya made me Beta on one condition. She made me promise that, if I ever felt in my heart of hearts that something she was doing was wrong, I must question her. I took that oath of course, but in all the years since that day, I have never once needed to make good on it.

I manage to get between them.

"Stop this!"

"It appears you have no control over your members, Freya."

"Chrissie, please. There's no need to worry."

"This is wrong Juliette," I protest. "Whatever happens, you lose. Can't you see that? Even if you could beat her, we won't follow you. We'll fight you to the death."

"That is a distinct possibility."

Her calm arrogance makes me want to slap her in the face.

"But then again," she says, "I never said anything about a fight. Freya can simply hand over the reins to me. It's been done before. What do you say, Freya? It would save everyone an awful lot of trouble."

"That's never going to happen," she snarls back.

"I guess a fight it is, then. And when we're done, and I've won, these lovely chaps here will scour the forest for your daughter. I assume that's where you told her to run? It would be the sensible thing to do. It is a big place. But they are known for their patience. I guess that comes with having all the time in the world."

The vampires have left their vehicles now and are standing in a row behind her. All nine of them, fangs bared and ready.

For the first time, a hint of fear flashes across Freya's face as she turns to me.

"Make sure—"

"I promise they'll never get near the forest," I interrupt.

I want to hug her. I want to tell her to beat this bitch back to the 1980s, where she and her Annie Lennox haircut should have stayed. But in that moment, Freya disappears, and in her place is the most beautiful wolf I have ever known. She always looks majestic, but in this moment, in this light, she seems almost ethereal.

"Go!" I turn to the others. "Change and—"

My words are cut short by the loud crack of gunshot originating from up in the hills. When the screaming starts, I realise what it was.

It takes me a moment to recognise it for what it is.

I turn back. There on the ground, the white wolf lies crumpled, blood flowing from a bullet wound to her head. I drop to my knees beside her.

"No!!!"

"Well, it's not the way I would have gone about it," Juliette comments, "but I guess we can all agree—I win."

EPILOGUE

Narissa

I don't know how long I've been running. Ten minutes? An hour? I can't tell. And I've no idea how far I've come. My wolf legs haven't let me down, even though my every instinct is to turn around and go back.

How could I have left? Part of me knows they will all be fine. She will be fine. As an untrained wolf, I took down a dozen vampires as if it were second nature. But none of this is their fault. It all comes down to me.

We're nearly there. Lou's voice is in my head. *Not long now. You'll make it.*

And then what? I want to reply. Just wait? My voice isn't in her head, yet she somehow knows what I'm thinking.

Trust Calin. He will meet you there and he will have a plan.

Can you hear him?

No. I need to double back and check the others have covered your scent. You know where you're going now. Just follow the tree line. It's not far.

Okay, I'll see you there. Be safe.

I will.

I've run for hours as a wolf before, but never like this, in fear of my life. Adrenaline is the only thing that's keeping me going. Was this how it was for Freya? No, I guess not. She didn't have a hoard of murderous vampires on her tail.

Paws burning, lungs fit to burst, I arrive at the meeting place and all but collapse. It's just as my mother described, a tiny clearing at the end of a dirt track, nothing special. I don't know whether to stay wolf or turn human. The knowledge that I'm in the very place they were together when my dad rescued my mother, decides the issue for me.

"Narissa, thank God."

I spin around.

"Calin!"

"Are you okay?"

"Yes, but what about Freya and the others?"

"I don't know. I left straight after you. I couldn't risk word getting back that I was here. But Freya will be fine. Your mother could take on the whole Council single-handed. I'm sure of it."

He can see that I'm still worried.

"I'll go back," he says, "as soon as you're gone and the vampires have left."

I go to hug him but stop, as I register what he's just said.

"What do you mean, when *I'm* gone? You're coming with me, aren't you? I don't even know where I'm supposed to be heading."

"Don't worry, it won't be long now. Just a couple of minutes."

I'm too exhausted to communicate all the questions racing through my mind, like when will I see him again. *If* I will see him again.

"Will you make sure she's safe?" is all I can manage.

"Of course I will."

"You promise?"

"I will do everything I can."

"Will you go back to London?"

"I have to."

I nod. "This is going to be a war, isn't it? Vampires versus werewolves."

"Not while I'm still standing."

I hear the sweet sincerity in his voice and wonder where I would be now if it had been another vampire's feeding docket I'd stolen from Oliver. Calin saved me from my old boss and his thugs, then at the Blood Bank and again when the vampires had me in their dungeon. I want to thank him for everything he's done for me.

Suddenly, a collective howl fills the air. It's coming from the direction of the forest. No, it's further away than that. The village!

Panic rises in me. "What's happened? I need to change back to speak to the others."

"No." He grabs my arm. "We don't have time. He's nearly here."

"What do you mean? Who's nearly here?"

"Step back, quickly."

He pulls me away to the edge of the clearing.

At first, I can only hear the dreadful howling from the village but then there's a distant, thump, thump, thump, coming from the opposite direction. The sound grows in intensity until, suddenly, there's a terrible roaring noise. Dust and leaves are flying all around us. I screw my eyes up and cover my ears.

"Go!"

Calin points towards the helicopter that has just landed, only feet away from where we had just been standing.

"Go! He'll look after you. I've told him what to do."

"Who?"

A door slides open. At first, I can't see through the debris that's corkscrewing into the air. Then I see the face I'd recognise anywhere.

"Oliver!"

"Now go!"

Calin pushes me forwards, but my feet drag in the dirt. I don't want to go. I don't want to run away. I want to stay here. I want to exist in a time bubble with my mother and the pack—and him.

"Calin—"

"I'll contact you," he says, taking my hands and planting a kiss on my head. "We'll speak soon, but now you must leave."

Every part of me is numb.

I stagger towards the helicopter.

How will Narissa react to the news of her mother's death? Will Oliver be able to protect her from what she has unleashed? For these answers and more, pick up Dark Deception, Book 3 in the Dark Creatures Saga now!

SCAN ME

Wondering how how Freya and Michael met? Claim your collection of FOUR prequel novellas and discover what she was forced to do. PLUS, get information on new releases and exclusive content.

NOTE FROM ELLA

First off, thank you for taking the time to read **Dark Destiny**, Book 2 in the Dark Creatures Saga. If you enjoyed the book, I'd love for you to let your friends know so they can also experience this action-packed adventure. I have enabled the lending feature where possible, so it is easy to share with a friend.

If you leave a review **Dark Destiny** on Amazon, Goodreads, Bookbub, or even your own blog or social media, I would love to read it. You can email me the link at ella@ellastoneauthor.com

Don't forget, you can stay up-to-date on upcoming releases and sales by joining my newsletter, following my social media pages or visiting my website www.ellastoneauthor.com

ACKNOWLEDGMENTS

First off thank you to Christian for his amazing covers for the whole series and Carol for her diligent editing.

To Lucy, Kath and all the alpha and beta readers who have helped shape this novel, I'd be lost without you.

And lastly, thank you to all of you readers out there for taking a chance on my book. I hope it has bought you as much joy reading it as it did for me writing it.

Printed in Great Britain
by Amazon